"Caitlin!" called a female voice from the beach.

I walked down the flagstone path and peered over a six-foot drop. Below me, a woman rose from the waves. With the light behind her, she was a dark, mysterious figure — an alien being rising from an alien element. In one smooth motion, she raised her hands to wring the water from her hair, then began to walk toward me out of the ocean. All at once, goosebumps broke out all over my body. Whether it was the suddenness with which she had just *appeared* there in the water, or the fact that she seemed utterly at home in it, I was gripped by the beauty of this image. One part of me knew I was seeing only Perry in a wetsuit, but another part of me — the part of me that longs for beauty in a banal world — saw something else. I saw a strong woman having made herself one with courage, competence, and grace. I saw a warrior. And I felt joy.

LAUREN WRIGHT DOUGLAS

The Daughters of Artemis

NAIAD
1991

Printed in the United States of America on acid-free paper
First Edition

Edited by Christine Cassidy and Katherine V. Forrest
Cover design by Catherine Hopkins
Typeset by Sandi Stancil

Library of Congress Cataloging-in-Publication Data

Douglas, Lauren Wright, 1947–
    The daughters of Artemis : a Caitlin Reece mystery / by
Lauren Wright Douglas.
        p.   cm.
    ISBN 0-941483-95-9 : $8.95
    I. Title.
PS3554.O8263D38   1991
813'.54--dc20
                                                            91-25256
                                                            CIP

For Martha

About the Author

Lauren Wright Douglas was born in Canada in 1947. She grew up in a military family and spent part of her childhood in Europe. She published her first short story at age twelve in the school newspaper, and since then has pursued a part-time writing career. To support this avocation, she has been a high school English teacher, a French translator, a college English instructor, a creative writing teacher for gifted high school students, a public relations person, and a grant writer. Lauren moved from Oak Bay, Victoria, British Columbia to the American Southwest some years ago where she now lives with her partner and an ever-changing number of cats. Lauren's second Caitlin Reece novel, *Ninth Life,* won the 1990 Lambda Literary Award for Lesbian Mystery. She is presently at work on her fourth Caitlin Reece novel, *A Tiger's Heart,* which will be published by Naiad Press in 1992.

BOOKS BY LAUREN WRIGHT DOUGLAS

CHAPTER ONE
Monday

Late night phone calls scare me witless. In my experience, they mean nothing but bad news. A car plunges over a cliff, a plane drops from the sky, a heart stops: burdens too great to carry through the narrow door of morning. All must be told now, transferred onto other shoulders, made bearable by sharing. This burden was no different.

"Caitlin, it's Sandy." The Scottish burr on the other end of the line belonged to my good friend

1

Detective Sergeant Gary Alexander of the Oak Bay Police Department.

"Mmmph," I managed, sitting up and swinging my legs over the side of the bed. I snapped on the light and looked at the clock. Just after one. "Okay, I'm awake. What?"

"Now, be calm. I've something to tell you."

Be calm — was he kidding? After that particular admonition, my heartbeat accelerated by about fifty percent. "Your wife, is she —"

"It's nothing like that," he broke in. "It's Sean Macklin."

"Who?"

"Wake up and listen to me, lass. It's Sean Macklin. He's out. He's free."

Sean Macklin. I woke up. And remembered. Sweet-faced Sean Macklin. Soft-voiced Sean Macklin. Kidnapper and rapist Sean Macklin. Sick Sean Macklin. When I worked in the Crown Prosecutor's office, back in the days when I believed in justice with a capital J, Macklin was one of my first solo victories. Almost six years ago I had sent him away for a dozen years. Or so I'd thought. "What in hell is he doing out?"

"Och, the silver-tongued bastard," Sandy said in disgust. "He talked his way into some experimental rehab work-release program. He's been a good boy, so he's out."

"Of course he's been a good boy!" I shouted. "There aren't any women for him to victimize in prison. For God's sake, Sandy. He can't be out. He can't be!"

"Nevertheless, out he is. And he's going home."

"Damn it to hell!" I grabbed the phone and

leaped off the bed. Home was Saanich. Home was where his victim lived. Macklin had threatened both me and Sandy as he was dragged away from the courtroom, but he had saved his really creative threats for his victim. "Did you notify Wendy Murdoch?"

"I've tried," he said. "There's no answer. So I called you. Our mole in the prison hospital just came on shift. He's been hearing rumors about Macklin's being released and sure enough, they let him out. This afternoon, if you please."

"Oh, Jesus, Sandy. Isn't *anyone* from the prison going to call Wendy Murdoch?"

"Apparently not," he said. "And the Saanich cops aren't interested. Mr. Macklin hasn't done anything, has he? He has every right to go home. And Saanich is out of my jurisdiction, so I ought to keep my nose out of it. But I've got a bad feeling about this. And I thought you . . . well, you do these kinds of things now . . ."

"I'll take care of it," I told him, fear squeezing my heart. "Can you pull her address from your files?"

"I already did. Seven-fifty-three Lochside."

"I'm leaving right now," I told him. "And keep phoning." I didn't wait to hear his reply.

I peeled off my sweat bottoms, tugged on jeans, socks, and sneakers, and grabbed my .357 and a speedloader from the box in my closet. At a dead run, I plucked my windbreaker from the coat tree, slammed the front door behind me, and threw myself into the front seat of my MG. She's forty minutes away, I told myself. Maybe forty-five. You can make it. And you *will* make it because you bloody well

3

have to. I floored the accelerator and roared off to the highway.

Seven-fifty-three Lochside was dark and quiet. So were the neighboring houses. In fact, the whole damned street looked tucked in for the night. A small, white frame bungalow, Wendy Murdoch's home sat on a rather large lot, a sidewalk bisecting the neat yard. A streetlamp on the corner enabled me to see a couple of lawn chairs and a wicker cat bed on the wide, covered front porch. Parked on the gravel driveway was an elderly gold Datsun.

I took a deep breath and eased the MG's door open. Patting the .357 clipped to my jeans, I crouched, running from the shadows across several lawns, and around the back of seven-fifty-three. A kitchen window spilled a wedge of yellow light onto the darkened grass, and I looked around for something to stand on. Upending a metal bucket I found near a coil of hoses, I placed it just below the window and, balancing on one foot, peered cautiously above the sill. A small, dark-haired woman in a blue terry cloth robe sat at a pine table, a ceramic mug in one hand, a pencil in the other. An open textbook and a yellow legal pad lay on the table in front of her, the pad half-covered with notes. Clearly, she was studying. And just as clearly, she was alone. I almost fainted from relief. But why hadn't she answered her phone when Sandy called?

Jumping down from my perch on the bucket, I went around to the front door and knocked. In a moment the light went on, and a face peered at me

4

through the glass. I heard the sound of a deadbolt, and then the door opened a crack.

"Yeah?"

"Wendy, it's Caitlin Reece. You may not remember me, but I prosecuted Sean Macklin six years ago."

The door opened a little wider. "It *is* you," she said. "Hey, you sure look different."

"Yeah, well, I don't work for the CP's office any more. And I just got out of bed. Listen, I have to talk to you."

Fear made her prescient. "It's him, isn't it? Macklin. He's coming to get me, just like he said he would."

I equivocated, not wanting to scare the daylights out of her. "I don't know about that," I said. "But he's out."

"Come on in," she said grimly.

Fifteen minutes later, I came up from checking the phone in the basement, wiping my hands on my thighs. Wendy met me at the top of the stairs. She had changed into jeans and a sweatshirt. I didn't blame her. Pajamas make me feel vulnerable, too.

"That phone is okay, too," I told her. "The trouble has to be outside."

I took the flashlight she gave me and went down the back porch steps, hunting for the place where the phone line came into the house. I hunkered down and shone my light carefully up and down the wire. It took a minute, but I found what I was looking for. At about knee height, the line had been cleanly snipped and some kind of tiny high-tech gizmo no bigger than the first joint of my finger had been fastened to the bottom piece of the line. I was willing to bet that this gadget closed the phone circuit and prevented the telltale busy signal that a cut line otherwise gives. I decided to leave it in place for the cops. Damn it all. I had been nursing an irrational hope that Macklin would have forgotten about Wendy. And about me, too. No chance.

Suddenly I felt keenly, mortally vulnerable. When had he done this and where the hell was he? Behind a bush out there in the darkness? My skin itched at the thought of it. I forced myself to stand upright, telling my protesting brain I did *not* look like a target. Loping for the back door, I tore it open, slammed it shut, then locked it after myself.

"Pack your bags," I told Wendy. "The phone line's been cut."

To her credit, she didn't ask a single question. Within three minutes she was packed and ready. We met back in the kitchen.

"Do you have somewhere to go? People you can stay with?"

"Yeah. Some friends of mine at work."

I had this twitchy feeling between my shoulder blades. If I were a gambling person, I would have bet big money that the rehabilitated Mr. Macklin would pay this place another visit. Soon. After all, he needed to follow up on the severed phone line. My only surprise was that he hadn't already done so. But Wendy deserved a large break from fate. Maybe this was it. I looked around the kitchen. "Don't leave your address book there by the phone," I told her.

"Right." She stuffed it in a bag. Then she ran into the dining room, returning with a small armful — a brown leather notebook, the BC Tel white and yellow pages, and some smaller directories. "I write numbers and addresses all over the place," she explained.

"Whatever," I said. "C'mon now. You drive your car. I won't be right behind you, but I'll be following. If I pass you and honk, or pull up and flash my lights, pull over. Got it?"

She nodded. "Caitlin, I'm scared," she said, as if she had a monopoly on the emotion.

There was no time to be kind. "I know you are," I told her. "Just do it anyway."

When Wendy turned onto the coast road, I hung back for as long as I could without losing her, but no other car appeared. So I fell in behind, the Datsun's red taillights preceding me like a pair of demon's eyes in the dark. The ocean was on our right — the sleek, rippled pelt of a monstrous ebony beast, tipped here and there with silver. A full moon hung in the night sky, and by its light the road stretched ahead like a giant haberdasher's ribbon tossed carelessly over the hills.

When we reached Sidney about fifteen minutes later, I followed Wendy to a modest brick house near the water. I pulled into the gravel driveway after her and got out. She ran to the door and knocked vigorously. After a few moments, two women stood in the doorway and, as Wendy spoke a few words to them, they embraced her. I walked to the bottom of the steps, relieved. My work was done for tonight. One of the women walked with Wendy over to the Datsun, collected some of her belongings, and hurried back inside. While Wendy dug around on the back seat, the other woman came down the steps and looked at me appraisingly. She had frizzy blonde hair and a lavender wool sweater over red plaid pajamas. Tall and stocky, she frowned at me, arms crossed.

"Wendy was going to sell her house this summer," she said. "Dammit, this isn't fair. Why can't you guys do things right? This stinks."

Tell me about it, I thought. Then, stung, I said, "Hey, Wendy isn't the only one who has to scurry around watching her tail. Macklin threatened me and the cop who finally brought him in. We're all going to be looking over our shoulders. And for your information, I'm no longer part of the legal system. I'm a private detective."

"Thanks, Caitlin," Wendy said, coming up and taking my hands. "You probably saved my life."

"Call the police first thing tomorrow," I told her. "Tell them to go out there and take a look at the phone wire. They'll help." I looked from her to her friend. "But sooner or later, you'll have to go back. When you do —"

"She's not going back," the blonde stated.

"Viv, I *have* to," Wendy said sensibly. "For clothes and so on. To pack up. You know."

"Hmmf," Viv grunted.

"When you go back," I repeated to Wendy, "take someone with you. Viv, maybe."

Viv brightened at that. I sensed she'd like to go a few rounds with Macklin.

"And be careful driving back there. If he's hanging around, you don't want to lead him right to you." I scribbled my phone number on a piece of

8

paper and handed it to her. "Call me if you have any trouble."

"People like us can't pay your prices," Viv declared, as if penury were a virtue. "A private eye? C'mon. We're not rich." She gave me a smug smile, full of secret knowledge. "Anyway, you don't need to worry about Wendy. We're going to take her to some people who'll be only too happy to help her. For nothing."

Oh sure. I decided to ignore the big blowhard. Turning, I took Wendy by the shoulders. "Listen to me," I said gently. "You call me if you need me. For anything."

"But, what Viv said about money is true," she told me earnestly. "We all work at the mill. I only make nine-fifty an hour."

"This is on me. As far as I'm concerned, it's unfinished business."

CHAPTER TWO
Tuesday

When I finally rolled out of bed, it was well past noon. I hauled myself upright, feeling groggy, fuzzy-tongued, and disoriented. Yawning, I wrenched open the curtains to find a brilliant blue in progress outside. No doubt the rest of the world was already engaged in enterprises of great pith and moment while I had been catching up on my zzz's. Well, what the heck. That was why I was in business for myself, right? No time clocks to punch, no supervisors to placate, no mechanical, mind-numbing work to resent. And no weekly paychecks coming in. Ah, the delights of self-employment.

The cats were a gray and tabby island in a lake of butterscotch sunshine. I felt them there at the foot of my bed, recharging their batteries. Then, yawning again, I walked around the house, opening the curtains and a few of the windows. Measuring out coffee, I put the Krupps to work. A quick shower took care of the thick feeling in my head, and I pulled on some clean jeans and a comfy old red T-shirt with Dirty Harry's famous utterance on the front. As I wandered into the living room, toweling my hair dry, I caught a glimpse of myself in the mirror. I looked tired. A tallish woman with eyes somewhere between gray and green, hair somewhere between red and brown, mouth set in a weary half-smile. Was it possible that I could no longer gallivant all over Vancouver Island, staying out half the night doing battle with the Forces of Evil, without showing some fraying around the edges? Some unraveling of seams? *After all, you are about to be forty,* a snotty little voice reminded me. *Perhaps you ought to act your age. Oh yeah?* I retorted, baring my teeth at myself in the mirror. *Aren't we told life begins at forty? Hmmm? Or are the wags wrong?* The voice was wisely silent.

In the kitchen I poured coffee and considered the afternoon. I had intended a day of R & R before my new client interview at seven that evening. No newspaper, no phone calls, no television, no radio. I had wanted to listen to Purcell and read poetry. Instead, I would now have to deal with Sean Macklin. Rehabilitated, my ass. A rehabilitated Sean

11

Macklin was a contradiction in terms. An oxymoron. You know, like government intelligence, or jumbo shrimp, or men at work. I put a bagel in the toaster and picked up the phone to dial Sandy's number.

"That little swine!" Sandy swore after I had told him of the results of my early morning adventure. "You know, of course, that there's nothing we can do. Officially."

"Yeah, I know. But that doesn't mean much, does it? Look what the brain trust up at the prison did, *officially*. I wonder if they pulled Macklin's jacket, read what he actually did to his victims. Dammit, Sandy, don't they have wives and daughters? And pets?"

I could hear him sigh. "Who knows?"

"I don't know about you," I told him, "but I'm not going to sit quietly with my hands folded, waiting for Mr. Macklin to adjust *my* phone line."

"Caitlin," he said admonishingly.

"Yeah, yeah, I know. But don't be so self-righteous, Alexander. Remember, you're on his hit list too. I have a right to be a trifle excited about this. Once he learns that Wendy has been spirited away, on whom, pray tell, do you think he's going to vent his spleen? Shit, Sandy, I don't want to sound paranoid but he *did* promise to cut my heart out right after he removed Wendy's. Yours comes next, I recall."

"Och, what a balls-up," he said.

"You can say that again, my friend. So what do we do? Unofficially, of course."

He exhaled heavily.

"Want to take a little drive with me later this afternoon? Out to Saanich?"

"Caitlin," he said again, in that tone of warning.

"I know, I know. You can't. Officially or unofficially. That's why you're such a good cop. But I believe I might take a little spin up the peninsula. A fact-finding mission, so to speak. Do we know if Macklin's gone back to his mother's house?"

"That's the address the prison has for him. But Caitlin . . ."

"What?"

"Ah, Caitlin, why do you want to do this?" he asked. "It'll only cause more trouble. I can almost smell it. Macklin's as crafty as a weasel — we both know that."

Now it was my turn to sigh. "Listen, Sandy, let's be clear on this. I don't *want* to do it. But I can't not go. Does that make any sense to you?"

"Of course it does," he said sadly. "Haven't I known you for ten years?"

"About that, I guess," I said gruffly.

"Call me," he said. "And be very bloody careful."

Alice Macklin's house didn't look like the lair of a beast. It was a rather ordinary two-story cedar shingle home, a pair of stubby-fingered monkey trees gracing the front yard, neat flowerbeds under the windows. On this brisk, bright March afternoon the street was deserted. Presumably everyone was at work or at play indoors. I wondered what the reformed Mr. Macklin was up to after a heavy night of prowling the countryside. Jesus. That had been his first night of freedom: who knew what tonight would bring.

I extracted my bogus *Victoria Times Colonist* business card from my wallet and marched up to the front door. Alice Macklin answered on my third knock. The six years since Macklin's trial had not exactly been kind to her. Fretting over the well-being of her "boy," as she persisted in calling him, had turned her from a self-possessed, aristocratic-looking forty-four year old to a thin-faced, harried fifty year old with wary eyes and graying hair. Realizing you have a monster for a son can do that to you, I supposed.

I wondered if Macklin was living in the room downstairs, the room with the separate entrance and bathroom, the room where he had kept the mementos of what he had done: Polaroid pictures of all his victims, lovingly arranged in five photo albums. His earliest prey had been kittens at age eleven; his latest, Wendy Murdoch at age twenty-three. I wondered if the psychiatrists up at the prison had leafed through those albums. I guessed not.

"Yes," she said tentatively, a tall, pathetically thin woman in a white sweater and black polyester slacks.

"I'm from the newspaper," I told her brightly, waving my business card under her nose. "Dr. Rosenblatt up at the prison gave us Sean's name. We're doing a series on rehabilitated felons, you see, and he thought Sean would make a wonderful —"

"He's not home," she interrupted. "He's at work." I knew that — a phone call earlier had confirmed his absence. "This is his first day on the job," she offered.

"Really?" I said brightly. "Gosh, that's just the

kind of information I need. The readers will love it. Do you think you could spare me a few minutes?"

"Well . . . I don't know . . ."

"It'll hardly take any time at all," I assured her. "And we *do* want to present Sean in the best possible light, now don't we?"

She looked at me wistfully, wanting to believe. "All right then. If it won't take very long." She opened the door and invited me into a large, modestly furnished living room. "Please, sit down." She crossed the room quickly to close the kitchen door. But not quickly enough. I saw the bottle of Gilbey's gin sitting on the table, the half-full glass beside it, and despite my vow not to feel sympathy for her, I felt a pang, sharp as steel, for Alice Macklin.

"I'd like to focus on his job," I lied. "You know, how he's going to fit into the mainstream of life. That sort of thing."

She patted her hair. "Well, he took some tech classes at the prison shop — marine engine repair, welding, and so on. He did very well." Her eyes were full of pain. "He's smart." I recalled how, during the trial, it came out that she had had hopes of Sean's becoming an attorney. He was certainly smart enough, but he had charmed his way through school, ending up knowing nothing, sabotaging every chance to make something of himself. When his eleventh-grade English teacher, a tough old bird named Moira Peters, wouldn't give him a pass, he threw a Molotov cocktail through her front window. The fire did several thousand dollars worth of damage to the interior. And the cops never caught who did it. But Moira Peters knew who did it, and

Sean knew that Mrs. Peters knew. To her credit, she still didn't pass the little bastard. So he quit school and devoted himself full-time to making himself an adept of the black rites of suffering. It took him three years to get caught. Wendy Murdoch and I caught him.

I used to think that guys like Sean — and they are all guys — were products of the mixed messages we give boys as we try to socialize them to fit into genteel society. But now I think, corny as it sounds, that they're evil. I think they know the difference between right and wrong as well as any of us, but they simply choose to do wrong. Because they want to. Because they can. Because that's the way they are. Once you admit that evil exists, everything else follows. I had seven years of firsthand experience with evil. I saw it, interviewed it, wrestled with it. And I'm no closer now to understanding it.

"Where is Sean working?" I asked Alice Macklin.

"At the Saanich Marina. He's got a job in the shop. Working on boat motors."

We chatted for a while after that, and I pretended to take notes, but I had what I wanted: his place of employment. And I got the name of one of his friends, too. With difficulty, I pried myself away from Mrs. Macklin. Despite what she had said, she really did want to talk. She wanted desperately to convince herself that it was all over, that Sean really *was* rehabilitated. I felt another stab of pity for her as I rose to leave, but reminded myself that she had been one of the chief apologists for Sean. His childhood pastimes of animal-torturing and fire-setting had just been phases, she had stoutly maintained throughout his trial. He was really a good boy. He'd straightened out. Uh huh.

I drove thoughtfully to the Saanich Marina, noting with interest that it was just across the bay from Wendy Murdoch's house. Coincidence? Not a chance. I was willing to bet that Macklin had picked this marina as a prospective place of employment, then charmed someone at the prison into getting him a job there. Well, tough luck, Macklin my boy. Your prey has flown. Although I realized after a heartbeat what he'd probably do when he saw he'd been thwarted: come after me.

The marina was quiet this time of year. Activity would heat up in a couple of months, once boating season really began. But now, in March, it was almost dead.

I ambled down the asphalt path from the parking lot to the water and admired the boats tied up at the docks. A pretty sight. Then I looked around the office. I spied a salt-bleached shingled two-story structure perched at the edge of the water and made my way over there. A couple of thirty-foot motor sailers had been hoisted out of the water and were hanging in heavy canvas slings, awaiting bottom work, I supposed. On a platform under one of them, a slim young guy in gray coveralls, a shock of black curls vivid against pale skin, worked on a motor. I squinted. Could be.

The Personnel Office was easy to find — a sign on the door saved me any serious detecting. A sweet young blonde thing in jeans and a pink wool sweater, her hair tied back with a pink ribbon, looked up as I approached. The nameplate on her desk said Melissa Donovan.

"Can I help you?"

"Yes, you can," I said, trying my best to look stern. "I'm from the Department of Corrections." Her blue eyes widened.

"Oh no. Is it about Sean?"

"Well, sort of. We're just, you know, keeping tabs on him. We really want him to have the best possible chance to succeed."

"Oh, he will," she said stoutly.

I groaned. Evidently Macklin had been practicing his charm on Melissa. "Is he here today?"

"Sure," she said, getting up to look out the window. "Right there, under the motor sailer. He was on time, too," she volunteered.

"Thanks," I said. "I'll just go on out and have a word with him. It's good to know he has such a rooting section." Melissa blushed. "Oh, by the way, did he tell you what he served his time for?"

"No," she said, looking virtuous. "And none of us asked, either. My dad told us not to — he's in charge of hiring and so on. He believes that what's done is done. Sean served his time and deserves the same chance as anyone else to make a living, Dad says."

Oh, Melissa. How could I tell her they had a viper in their midst?

"Thanks," I said, and left, feeling sick.

Outside the marina office, I put on my sunglasses, walked down the path, and stood for a moment, looking down at the toiling Sean Macklin. He had changed position, and now I had an excellent view. His face was set, intent, and I noted that the six years since I had last seen him had left him all but untouched. He still looked twenty — smooth, unlined skin, guileless blue eyes, long, black eyelashes, cheeks that looked as though they never needed shaving, pretty red lips. I wondered how he had survived in prison. Probably as someone's bunkmate. Sighing, I walked back thoughtfully to my car. I had done what I intended — run him to ground and brushed up on the visual details necessary to activate the Sean Macklin file in my brain. Now I wanted to go home.

CHAPTER THREE

Among the joys of self employment is the phenomenon of too little time to do too much. I ended up spending the rest of the day on paperwork, not Purcell. So when six-thirty rolled around, I found that I would just have time for a quick sandwich, and then I would have to run to my apartment. Rummaging in the fridge, I found a package with a couple of slices of turkey that still smelled okay, and the end of a loaf of whole wheat bread. Slapping my meager meal together, I hurried to the bedroom to change. Somehow I didn't think that my *Go ahead, make my day!* T-shirt was quite the thing for my client interview tonight. It might give my prospective employer the wrong idea about me. Although, I thought, as I tossed the T-shirt on a chair and pulled an inoffensive gray turtleneck over my head, maybe not.

It took me fifteen minutes to drive to the university. I got out of my car and was just zipping up my windbreaker when I heard something. Or thought I did. Alone in the ill-lighted parking lot, I froze, heart thudding. Had that been a scream? Shouldn't I check it out? My shadow lay on the asphalt ahead of me, an attenuated ghoulish finger pointing toward the darkened park. I swallowed, mouth dry. But although I waited, motionless for perhaps two minutes, the sound was not repeated. I let out a breath I hadn't realized I'd been holding.

A lone gull swooped by at streetlamp level and I relaxed. Perhaps the sound I had heard had been only a bird's cry. Or the wind moaning in the oak trees. I shrugged and headed for the dark path that led across the small campus park to my destination: the cheerful neon glimmer of shops and restaurants on the university's south edge. If I weren't such a cheapskate, I'd go on over to Arbutus Street and pay for parking, but I've been parking gratis at U Vic for years. Old habits die hard.

I heard them before I saw them — several people marching in aggressive unison. More curious than alarmed, I continued down the path. We met at the streetlight where various walkways intersected like the hub of a wheel, about halfway to Nootka Hall. Arms linked, three women swept down on the intersection like a force of Furies. I was more than a little taken aback — these ladies evidently meant business. What kind, I wasn't sure. Their white wool berets and white armbands bearing insignia of some kind gave them a paramilitary look. Something stirred in my memory: hadn't they been featured on the evening news recently? One of the marchers carried a very formidable-looking staff — as tall as she was and as big around as my wrist. I decided not to contest their right to the sidewalk and prudently stepped off into the grass, waiting for them to pass. The marcher in the middle, a six-foot redhead for whom the name Amazon might have been coined, brought the cadre to a halt under the streetlamp and eyed me speculatively.

"Need an escort?" she inquired, looking down at me. She was clad in a black wool cape which she cast off one shoulder with a dramatic flourish.

"No thanks," I replied, trying hard not to smile at how seriously she took herself. "I'm going on to Arbutus Street."

"That's clear across the park," the redhead said, frowning in evident disapproval. "Have you forgotten about the rapes?"

As a matter of fact, I had. Sean Macklin's nocturnal shenanigans had chased clean out of my mind the fact that we had had several rapes in the university area. "No," I lied patiently, "but —"

"But you think it can't happen to you, right?" she demanded, frowning. The Myrmidons flanking her frowned in unison.

I sighed, trying hard not to be irked. They're young, I told myself. Idealistic. But still, this was *my* safety they were talking about. I'd been accustomed to looking after myself for years now. Probably since before they were born. I forced myself to bite my tongue.

"Stephanie Hayes thought it couldn't happen to her," the redhead informed me. "So did Deena Wilson."

I said nothing.

The redhead shrugged, reached into the recesses of her cape and withdrew a piece of paper. Shoving it into my hands, she linked arms with her friends. "Read that," she ordered, and the three quick-stepped away.

I stuck the paper into the back pocket of my jeans, patted the comforting weight of the Smith and Wesson .357 Magnum clipped to my belt under my windbreaker, and continued on my way. But by now I had become positively skittish. Sean Macklin was bad enough. But thanks to the redhead, I now had the Full Moon Rapist, as the media had named him, on my mind too. Macklin had driven thoughts of the rapist out of my mind, but they now returned, reluctantly.

Since December, there had been two rapes and one attempted rape — three attacks in three months, always on the U Vic campus, always at the full moon. This pattern had led the press, always ready with a *bon mot,* to dub this man the Full Moon Rapist. Why lionize this vicious coward by giving him a romantic title? It only served to add a spurious glamor to what were, after all, particularly despicable assaults. We don't need any more homage to the myth of the heroic rapist.

I've noticed there is a curious doublethink associated with rape. And I believe the blame for this can be attributed directly to the baleful and mischievous influence of the gentlemen of the press. Why is it that men who rape and/or murder women are so often romanticized with fanciful sobriquets? Jack the Ripper, the Parking Lot Rapist, the Green River Killer, the Hillside Strangler, the Apologetic Rapist. I sometimes fear that there may be something in the male psyche that unconsciously applauds violence against women to such an extent that they find a gleeful satisfaction in bestowing glamorous titles on the perpetrators. I would like to be wrong about this, but I have yet to hear the press invent such colorful titles for men who go berserk and snipe from clock towers, or murder six of their family members, or drive their cars into crowds of pedestrians, or gun down a couple dozen diners at McDonald's. If my years in the Crown Prosecutor's office taught me anything, they taught me that woman-as-victim is still a titillating tune on far too many male hit parades.

The Full Moon Rapist indeed. I snorted and continued on my way.

Despite what I had said to the three-woman cadet review, I couldn't help feeling apprehensive. Although these are the bold, brave nineties, anxiety still walks with any woman who has to navigate dark, lonely places. Most of the time I managed to control the urge to look back over my shoulder; however, tonight I was keenly aware of it. So when an owl hooted in a Garry Oak, I almost levitated off the asphalt. Almost there, Caitlin, I told myself. People and bright lights are just around the corner.

The path made an abrupt right turn, paralleling the rear of Nootka Hall, and I felt better seeing the building's cheery yellow lights. Two uniformed security guards crunched toward me on the cinder path, one twisting the top of a flashlight. A spear of light shot out ahead of them, piercing the dark, and as they passed me, I felt the back of my neck prickle. Oh come off it, I chided myself. Don't be such an idiot. Then, directly ahead of me was Arbutus Street, the blinking neon and honking horns of civilization. I hurried to the end of the path and stood on the curb, waiting for a chance to dash through the traffic. A wind from the sea ran its fingers through my hair and I shivered a little in the cool night air of a Pacific Northwest March.

I opened the door of Meyer's Deli to a warm, humid tangle of aromas. Onions, pickles, garlic, smoked meat — all the ingredients of a really good case of halitosis. And heartburn. I fought the desire to lick my chops, won, and looked around the crowded shop for my client. She wasn't hard to spot.

Perry Eldon sat at a table against the wall, drinking that expensive brand of water that comes in green glass bottles. I studied her for a moment as I weaved my way through the gaggle of tables and chairs. Blonde curly hair, freckles, ruddy cheeks, wiry suntanned arms: she looked dismayingly like an advertisement for Good Clean Living. A well-washed blue T-shirt (with the sleeves rolled a little), honestly faded jeans, and worn running shoes also told me something about her: this was a lady who watched her pennies. A scuffed navy athletic bag with SWIM CANADA stenciled on it in white lay beside her on the floor. Hmmm. A college athlete?

As I approached, she left off picking at the remains of a fruit salad and looked up quickly. Recognizing me, she smiled. "Hi," she said

25

diffidently. "I'm glad to see you again. I'm just sorry it had to be under these circumstances."

"No problem," I told her, drawing my chair up to the table. A waiter materialized at my elbow and I ordered coffee, suppressing an almost overwhelming desire for a Montreal smoked meat sandwich. As the waiter ambled away, my stomach registered its disappointment with a particularly traitorous roar of protest. *Quiet, down there,* I told it sternly. *We've been thinking of dieting, remember? You've had your supper, so don't carry on as though you've never had a decent meal. Give me a little help here.*

Perry looked up at me and smiled tentatively. Her brown eyes and jet black eyebrows contrasted wonderfully with her blonde hair, but I forced my mind back to business and smiled encouragingly in return. She was plainly nervous, so I decided a little small talk wouldn't hurt.

"Still working at the Dog and Pony?" I asked her. This scrofulous local pub was where I had met Perry, almost nine months ago. She was slinging drinks and I was burning the midnight oil for the animal rights group Ninth Life, my client at the time.

She shook her head. "Not any more. I've got a job driving a truck for a delivery service. The hours are better. So's the pay. And the parcels in the van don't throw up on my shoes or try to come on to me."

My coffee arrived. I asked her, "Did you ever take that self-defense course?"

"No," she said, sighing. "I guess I got too busy."

"So, are you a college swimmer now?"

"What? Oh. No, I'm a triathlete. I just turned pro a few months ago and I'm training for a big competition. I use the U Vic pool sometimes."

I was impressed and wanted to hear more, but it was time to get down to business. "How can I help you, Perry?"

She ran a hand through her hair, then gave me a baffled glance. Anger and hurt looked briefly out of her eyes but she concealed those emotions almost immediately. "I don't know. I feel like a fool. In fact, I've been sitting here thinking I made a mistake asking you to come here. I'm probably wasting your time."

"How do you know? You haven't told me what you want me to do yet."

"Well, I've been to the police. They can't help me. So maybe no one can."

"If you believed that you wouldn't be here."

"I don't know," she said, sounding helpless. "I don't know anything any more."

I clammed up and decided to let her talk. Either she would get it out or she wouldn't.

"It's my sister," she said finally. "She's run away."

"Oh yeah? How old is she?"

"She's just a kid. She —"

"Perry, how *old* is she?"

"Eighteen."

I shook my head. "She's no kid. She's an adult. More than likely that's why the police don't want to get involved."

She grimaced in disgust.

"Was she kidnapped?"

"No."

"Is someone forcing her to do something against her will?"

"No."

"Is she into drugs?"

"No."

"Prostitution?"

"No."

"Well? What, then?"

She raised her eyes to mine, lips compressed to a thin line, jaw set, and I saw just how deep her anger went. Oho. Big sister was *extremely* pissed off at little sister. Interesting.

"You know," I said as gently as I could, "sometimes young people just up and run away. Especially the ones who've been model kids. Maybe she got bored out of her mind with her job or sick of her schoolwork. Maybe she was tired of you telling her what to do." Perry winced. Bull's eye. I continued, "Lots of kids go through periods like that. They're usually self-limiting."

"This isn't," Perry said through clenched teeth. "It's been going on for too long."

"Oh? How long?"

"About three months."

"She's been missing for three months?"

Perry made an impatient gesture. "She ran away not quite a month ago. When she turned eighteen. But she's been hanging around with this bunch of crazy people since Christmas or so."

"What crazy people?"

"Some women she met in one of her classes at U Vic. They live in some commune up by Land's End."

She raked her hair again. "I don't know much more about them than that."

"Have you been in touch with her? Asked her to come home?"

"I've tried!" Perry cried. "But she says she doesn't want to talk to me."

"Oh? Have you actually talked to her? Heard this from her yourself?"

"Yeah, I have. On the phone. Just before she moved up there. She was staying at a friend's house."

"Hmmm. What goes on at this commune? Are they back-to-nature types? Religious fanatics? Witches?"

"They're . . . oh hell, I don't know what they are. All I know is that they've got Tess." There was panic in her voice now. And I didn't believe her for a minute. I believed that she knew a lot more about them than she was telling me.

"What do you want me to do?"

Perry blinked, as if the truth should have been self-evident. "Talk to her, of course. Make her come home."

I held up a hand. "Whoa! I can most likely find her and talk to her, but I doubt I can make her come home."

"Why —" Perry broke off in evident frustration. "Damn it, she has to come home!"

"Have you thought of just waiting this out?"

"What do you mean?"

"Waiting for her to *want* to come home?"

Perry started to say something, then changed her mind. "Whether she wants to or not, she *has* to

29

come home," she said grimly. "I'm afraid these people are going to do something awful, something that will probably send them all to jail. Tess's . . . well, she doesn't really understand how serious this is, she —"

"How serious *what* is?" I asked in exasperation. "C'mon Perry, level with me. I can't help you if you're going to keep half the facts a secret."

"Shit," Perry said. Then, as if relieved that she'd put up a good fight but lost to a superior opponent, she capitulated. "All right. I guess I have to tell you what I know. It's not much, and it sounds crazy, but —"

She was not allowed to finish her sentence. The howl of sirens and the scream of rubber on asphalt drowned out her words. Two police cars and an ambulance, lights flashing, came rocketing down Arbutus Street and, without pausing, jumped the curb and tore down the path that led to Nootka Hall.

And in a burst of preternatural clarity, I heard again the sound I had heard as I stood in the dark parking lot. It hadn't been a seagull or the wind or an owl. It *had* been a scream. And watching the police cars and ambulance hurtle down the walk to Nootka Hall, I intuitively knew who had uttered that cry: the Full Moon Rapist's latest victim.

I turned to Perry to ask her something, but my question died on my lips. As if mesmerized, she stared out the window at the flashing lights that could be plainly seen behind Nootka Hall. She had turned pale under her tan and her freckles stood out like crumbs on a white tablecloth. Then, with an inarticulate cry, she grabbed her sports bag, jumped to her feet, and bolted from the restaurant.

I swallowed the rest of my now cold coffee, dug some change out of my jeans, and navigated my way to the phone. As I dialed the television station, I allowed myself the hope that the ambulance, the police cars, and the Channel 22 NewsEye van had all congregated on Nootka Hall for something other than what I feared.

"Production. Lorraine speaking," said the familiar, harried voice of Lorraine Shaver.

"It's Caitlin," I told her. "Just say yes or no. Is it the rapist?"

"Yes."

"Damn," I said. "Thanks."

I hung up the phone and leaned against the wall, looking at the ceiling tiles. The Full Moon Rapist. Something about this latest attack had driven Perry nuts. But what? Did she know something about him? A chill walked down my spine — did the sister know something about him? That seemed more likely. What *was* her sister mixed up in, I wondered? And for that matter, what was the Full Moon Rapist doing attacking now? I peeled back my sleeve and looked at my watch. The digital display showed 3-21. March 21. The moon wouldn't be full for another four days. What was going on here? Had he changed his pattern, or was this the work of a copycat? A copycat who couldn't read a calendar.

I decided to split. I didn't want to sit here in Meyer's, brooding — I had people who needed me at home. As for Perry, if she needed me, she had my number. I found myself half-hoping she wouldn't call, though. What kind of a job could I do for her when my mind was sure to be occupied with thoughts of Sean Macklin? I sighed. Life was just too bloody complicated.

At home — half of an up-and-down duplex on Monterey Street in Oak Bay — I parked and hurried up the steps to my front door, keys in hand.

Inside, I shed my windbreaker, rubbed my hands together briskly, and called for the boys. Gosh, I hadn't talked to them all day! "Front and center, guys," I said, being careful to position myself precisely in the middle of the oval braided rug in front of my coffee table. "The Servant of Cats has arrived."

"Nrraf?" inquired an eager tenor voice from behind an armchair. Almost immediately, my large gray cat Repo emerged from his nest in the mohair blanket I kept there, and began enthusiastically weaving between my ankles, butting his head on my shin. Repo — short for Repossessed — was the sole survivor of one of the university's psychology department learning experiments. Unfortunately Repo's fellow experimenters had learned a horrible lesson: if your keeper goes on holiday for two weeks and doesn't arrange for a replacement, you die. I bent to scratch his head and he swooned in ecstasy, collapsing at my feet like a felled fir.

"You're too easy," I said, nudging him affectionately with my foot. "Attila the Hun could scratch your ears and you'd follow him anywhere."

"Ruff," he agreed.

Then, from behind the chair came striding a slim, striped gentleman — my mackerel marvel, my serendipitous surprise, my sweet, blind Jeoffrey. Another refugee from scientific research, Jeoffrey had been blinded in the course of an unspeakably cruel joke in a cosmetics testing lab. Like Repo, he was lucky to be alive.

"Hi, guy," I whispered.

He looked up at me, unseeing golden eyes wide, and with a great display of confidence, marched straight to me. Standing on his hind legs, he stretched, putting his front paws on my knees. "Mrrrrr?" he asked in a decidedly seductive tone.

"You betcha," I told him, scooping him gently into my arms and draping him over one shoulder. "Say that to me once more and I'll go with you to the ends of the earth. Katmandu, even."

"Mrrrrr," he repeated breathily, nuzzling my cheek. I shivered deliciously. It's not everyone who has a cat who whispers sweet nothings in her ear.

"C'mon, Rotund One," I told Repo. "Let's see what mouth-watering delicacy we can scare up."

With surprising agility for one so portly, Repo leaped to his feet and preceded us smartly into the kitchen. There he positioned himself in a supervisory stance on the counter. I deposited Jeoffrey beside him and they sandpapered each other's ears and jowls with busy tongues while I surveyed the cat food scene. A quick check told me it was a choice between Little Bits O' Beef and Little Bits O' Beef.

"How about Little Bits O' Beef?" I inquired. They consulted briefly, then Repo, the spokescat of the pair, gave me his approval. "Yang," he agreed.

"An excellent choice, sir," I assured him, brandishing the can opener and scooping the cat food into two china dishes. I put the dishes down on the bright blue and white plastic CAT MAT on the floor, and lowered Jeoffrey to his bowl. Repo descended to the floor with a *whuff* and the two slurped and smacked their way through dinner.

I poured myself an ounce of Scotch and sat at the kitchen table, watching my cats, trying not to be depressed. But I felt moroseness enveloping me. The fragile bubble of safety inside which I lived had been popped, and I had become anxious and angry. Damn Sean Macklin and damn the Full Moon Rapist, too. I felt like a mongrel dog circling the lights of some little town, longing to feel that there was safety somewhere.

With a sigh, I went into the bedroom and put my gun away. I had just stowed it safely in its shoebox and walked into the hall to turn off the light when I saw an ominous glow from my study.

"Nuts," I said aloud and strode purposefully into the room. There, on a work table I had constructed from a door laid across two filing cabinets, reposed my new computer. Nothing ominous about that. Except it was on and I hadn't turned it on. Worse yet, there was a message on the screen. With sinking heart, I approached. The screen bore one line of glowing amber print:

<L>;;:zaxchssssbrtt

"Shit!" I yelled. This wasn't the first time this had happened. *Au contraire*, it was the third. The first two times a line of nonsense had appeared on

34

the screen, I had called the manufacturer's 800 number in a panic, certain that the machine was about to self-destruct. A young man who sounded about nine assured me that nothing was wrong. At least I think he assured me that nothing was wrong. I spoke English. He spoke RAM and ROM, bits and bytes.

Computers, and the people who sell and service them, intimidate the hell out of me. I would never have bought this sleek electronic *thing* for myself — the computer, a built-in modem, and a carload of software, were gifts from a grateful client. And the components had sat here, innocent and polite, just the way a good minion should, until last week. Then it started leaving me strange messages. At first I thought they were meaningful. Then I thought they were a joke. Now I've decided they're spooky. A kind of high-tech automatic writing. Voices from the void.

In exasperation, I punched the thing's power button and cleared the screen. Was it my imagination or did it heave a sibilant silicon sigh of disappointment as I sent its latest attempt at communication straight to electronic heaven? Give me a break! Who needs a haunted computer?

In fact, who needs a computer at all? I'm a bibliophile, a book lover. I'm hooked on the heft of books in my hands, the shapes of different typefaces, the feel of paper. I love books' covers. I love to see them lined up on my bookshelves.

I stood there looking at the brightly colored packages of software and despaired. From the shelf, I plucked *Aldus Pagemaker,* a desktop publishing program and snorted. Who but a reactionary like me would know, or care, that the original Aldus was

Aldus Manutius (1450–1515), a scurrilous but energetic Venetian publisher who probably had more to do with the Renaissance than anyone besides Gutenberg. He published all the extant Greek and Roman tracts, and he did something that endeared him to me. He realized that books need not be imitation manuscripts, they didn't need to be the same size and shape as the cumbersome, unwieldy manuscripts from which they were copied. They could be portable! It's no accident that books today are the size they are — they had to fit in a fifteenth century horse's saddlebags. That's one of my favorite personal metaphors for the accessibility of knowledge: you have to be able to hold it in your hands and fit it in a saddlebag. And the behemoth on my work table wouldn't fit in anyone's saddlebag.

I had just about decided that I ought to go to bed when the phone rang. It was Malcolm, one-half of my upstairs tenant duo.

"We were just watching the news on Channel Twenty-two," he said. "About the rapist. I remembered you had said that you were going over to the U tonight and we wondered, that is, we thought . . ."

I was touched. "I'm here and unscathed," I reassured him. Another woman couldn't claim such a fortunate fate.

"Yvonne's taking this hard," he told me, lowering his voice. "Something like this went on in Brisbane, just before we emigrated." A pause. "One of the victims was Yvonne's best friend Maureen. They never caught him." I could hear the quaver in Malcolm's voice. "Yvonne's, um, she's in the kitchen, baking — that's what she always does when she's

36

stressed. I was wondering if you could, well, come up and talk to her. Not necessarily about the rapes. Anything will do. I'm worried, Caitlin. She —" He broke off and cleared his throat: "She's stopped talking to me. It's as if *I'm* to blame. Because I'm a man, I guess."

"I'll be up in a minute," I told him.

The prospect of being useful cheered me immensely. I wasn't much of a psychologist but I could listen if Yvonne wanted to talk. I realized that I might have to sample some of her baking and thought with a guilty twinge of my resolution to diet. Ah well, such were the tribulations of life.

On my way out, I passed the full-length mirror and paused, reconsidering. Only this morning I had had to loosen my belt to get it comfortably fastened. That distressed me. And lately, my jeans had begun to feel tight. What was going on here? I exercised more or less regularly — swimming a mile three times a week was about all I could manage — and I never made a pig of myself at meals. So why this increasing girth? Was corpulence in my future? I made a face at myself and studied my image. When would it happen, I wondered. When was the official beginning of old age? The first gray hair? The first morning my joints protested getting out of bed? The first time I couldn't sling a fifty-pound bag of kitty litter onto my shoulder? Somehow I didn't think I would accept growing old with much grace. I patted my stomach. Well, maybe there was an ever so tiny bulge there. Was this it — the First Dire Sign of Aging? I grimaced, stood as tall as my five foot-eight would allow, and flexed my biceps. Whatever the reason, those extra pounds were coming off, I vowed.

I snapped out the light and marched toward the stairs.

"Delicious," I told Yvonne, licking the last crumbs of a third whole wheat cinnamon roll off my fingers.

"A little too brown," she said critically, inspecting the rolls as she eased them out of the pan and onto a plate. "I won't bake the next batch quite so long."

Malcolm rolled his eyes and fled to the living room. For my part, I took a stool from the dining room and came to sit beside Yvonne as she rolled out the dough, slathered it with oil, sprinkled it with brown sugar, cinnamon and raisins, and rolled it up. "You know," I said as I cut the dough into pinwheels, "I'm thinking of going on a diet. Can you recommend a good one?"

She huffed, and glanced over at me, raising a blonde eyebrow. "Diet? But Caitlin, you're not *fat!*"

"No, but my jeans are tight. I think that's a message from the Great Gourmand in the sky to cool it."

She huffed a little more. "You don't eat properly as it is," she reminded me. "Now you're going to go on some faddish diet and eat bananas for two weeks, or grapefruit, and, and —"

To my amazement, she began to sob, then to weep in earnest, and finally to wail. Hands covered with sugar and cinnamon, she clutched her hair and howled. I leaped off the stool, put my arms around her, and held her as tightly as I could. "Go ahead," I told her. "Scream your head off if you want to."

And she did. Malcolm put his head around the

corner of the kitchen door and, eyes round as blue marbles, left us to it. I held her as she wept for her friend Maureen, for herself, and for her rage at being made to feel afraid all over again. And as she cried, she beat my back and shoulders with her fists, hot tears running down the side of my neck and into my shirt. Finally her howls subsided to hiccupping sobs. "Caitlin," she whispered, "you must think I'm an idiot."

I shook my head and patted her shoulder reassuringly. "No. It's all right to be afraid. And angry."

"Not you, though," she said, stepping back from me. "You're not afraid, are you? You're never afraid."

No ma'am, certainly not. Not me. I thought about my moment of terror outside Wendy Murdoch's house, and felt conflicted, wanting to admit that hell, yes, I was afraid. Often. Instead, I decided to tell Yvonne what she seemed to need to hear. "No. I'm not afraid," I lied.

This seemed to satisfy her. "Oh look, Caitlin! You have cinnamon and sugar all over you," she wailed.

"Yeah. Tears, too. Who cares? These clothes were due for the laundry anyhow."

We laughed then, and she wiped her eyes with her shirt sleeve. "I'm going to wash my face," she said. "Want some tea?"

"Sure. As long as it's something sensible. None of those boiled roots and twigs you served me last time."

When she came back, scrubbed, hair brushed, she had a sheepish Malcolm in tow. "I found him hiding in the greenhouse," she said, "supposedly potting up some seedlings. Why don't you fill the kettle, Mal?"

she asked him. "I'll just put this last pan of rolls in to bake."

Malcolm looked at me hopefully and I gave him the thumbs-up sign. He sighed and began running the water.

When the tea had steeped — a sensible blend of Orange Pekoe — it was Yvonne who broached the subject of the rapes.

"The thing I will never forgive him for is that he's made me think about Maureen's ordeal and how obsessed I was with revenge. It passed, and I thought I'd never feel that way again. But I do. He's brought it all back." She looked belligerent.

Malcolm reached out tentatively and took her hand and I was relieved to see that she didn't snatch it away. They sat hand in hand, looking for all the world like siblings with their cornsilk blonde hair, delphinium blue eyes, and rosy cheeks. Expatriate Australians, they ran the local health food store and cafe, and over the years they had rented from me, we had become good friends. I had loaned them money to expand the health food store and they had paid the interest on the loan faithfully every month. In fact, they were just about to make the last payment on the principal. They were solid, steady, likeable people, and it hurt me to see them in distress.

"Did you prosecute many rapists?" Malcolm asked me.

"Yeah, a few. Nothing like the Full Moon Rapist, though."

"The men you prosecuted — did they go to prison?" Yvonne frowned at me.

I thought guiltily of Macklin. "Some did and

some didn't. Most rapes — apart from the ones that are characterized by irrefutable physical evidence — are still damned hard to prove. It's the old bugaboo of consent." I glanced at Yvonne, wondering just how much of this she wanted to hear. Not much, plainly, for her eyes had taken on a troubled, faraway look. I felt that she wanted a comforting summation — something that would make her feel safe, that would reassure her that no rapist ever escaped from me unpunished — but I couldn't give her one. The facts were the facts. I decided instead to take my leave.

"Gotta go," I told them, taking my dishes to the sink. "Thanks for the cinnamon rolls and tea."

Yvonne returned from her private deliberations with a start. "The rolls!" she exclaimed, making a lunge for the oven. "Oh no — they're burning!"

I winked at Malcolm and let myself out.

I tossed my clothes in the laundry basket, changed into my sweats-cum-pajamas, saw that Repo and Jeoffrey were comfy in the folds of their mohair nest behind my armchair, and took two fingers of Scotch into the bedroom with me.

I had intended to read — I'm halfway through Barbara Tuchman's *The March of Folly*, something I've always intended to read — but I didn't feel like any more folly right now. Instead, I propped myself up a little higher in bed, sipped my Scotch and thought about the question Yvonne had asked and I'd started to answer, about whether the rapists I prosecuted went to prison. Some had and some hadn't. And some, like Macklin, who until last night

I had counted among my victories, were cut loose by soft-headed psychologists. Talk about sabotage.

But most rapists were never convicted because of another kind of sabotage: our wonderful jury system. As a rookie in the CP's office I had been properly horrified at the low conviction rate we secured on rape cases. Because even though we might be able to prove the evidentiary requirements of force and resistance, juries are influenced hardly at all by bruises, and not at all by threats. They have only a dim understanding that just the *threat* of violence might be enough to terrorize a woman into submission — not into consent, but into compliance. And defense lawyers love compliance.

In criminal prosecutions, rape ranks second only to murder in the percentage of cases in which a defendant prefers to take his chances on a jury. And the defendants and their legal counsel are right. Juries are allies. Judges are made of sterner stuff, but juries are traditional allies of male defendants and enemies of female complainants for reasons that run deeper than their poor grasp of law or their predominantly male composition. Juries are composed of citizens who *still* believe many of the myths about rape and they judge females according to these myths.

Other than the fact of intercourse, the law recognizes only one issue in rape cases: whether there was consent at the moment of intercourse. But to my exasperation, I soon learned that the jurors in the cases I prosecuted did not limit themselves to this one issue. They went on to weigh a woman's conduct in the prior history of the affair. They closely and often harshly scrutinized the female complainant herself, and were moved to be lenient with the defendant whenever there were suggestions of "contributory behavior." These juries were rewriting the law, bootlegging concepts from tort law or civil law such as "contributory negligence" and "assumption of risk" and using them in rape cases. I was appalled. How could we ever win, I wondered. How could we ever convict? Because, apart from cases in which there was "extrinsic violence" — a wonderful, loaded term — juries accommodated the male defendant. In a law review article I read, in which judges were asked if they would have convicted these "simple rape" cases, they stated they would have done so in fifty-two percent of the cases. Yet the juries actually convicted only seven percent.

That statistic was unimaginably depressing. Questions like *Jesus, why do we bother?* had gone through my mind for weeks. And when my turn came, and I presented the best case I could and the defendant walked away, I felt that not only the law, but that I, personally, had failed the complainant. I learned the hard way that the deck is stacked against women in more ways than we ever dreamed, and when I finally left the Crown Prosecutor's office, my only regret was that I hadn't left earlier.

Fortunately, I no longer need give a rat's ass for juries or for the rules of evidence. Now, people come to me with problems which they can't get resolved within the system and I listen and decide if I think I can help them. Sometimes I can — because I operate in a very direct way. I've discarded such meaningless notions as "right" and "justice" and "fairness." Once I acknowledged that the thin blue line is not sufficient to keep the hordes of bad guys at bay, that good people will not necessarily prevail simply because they are right, I found I had an interesting choice to make. I could close my eyes and ears and get on with my own life, or I could try to help the decent folk who needed it. So I decided to hire out my wits, my strength, and my determination to assist those the system can't help.

I frowned and took the final sips of my Scotch. Some mean, unsporting part of me wanted to rub the bad guys' noses in failure, to show them that despite their guile, their cunning, their arrogance, and their preferential treatment under the law, they couldn't always count on winning. I wanted them to know that there are people like me willing to step between them and their victims, to doff the gloves of civilized behavior, and to fight them for their prey.

And over the years, I've garnered quite a few enemies. It makes me more than a little nervous to think that some of them harbor grudges against me, so I walk softly and carry a big .357. But all the Sean Macklins in the world won't make me stop doing what I'm doing. Because stopping them is always worth the price. And, as I get older, I suspect it may be the only thing worth doing.

Tsk, tsk. You're getting positively maudlin, Reece. Give it up for tonight and get some sleep. Exhausted by musings of such cosmic import, I put my glass down on the bedside table and turned out the light.

When the phone rang at one-thirty, I had an overwhelming feeling of *deja vu*. As I surfaced through layers of sleep, I imagined I'd hear Sandy's voice urging me to be calm. In the process of fumbling for the phone, I overturned a glass of water and skinned my knuckles on the clock radio. So I was in a less than agreeable frame of mind when I finally put the receiver to my ear.

"*What?*" I snapped.

"Caitlin, is that you?" It was Perry.

"Yeah."

"Listen, I'm sorry to call you at this hour. And I'm sorry I ran away like I did. But I had a reason," she rushed to assure me. "If you'll let me, I can explain. And what I said before is truer than ever now. I — Tess and I — need your help. Will you listen?"

I tried to flog my reluctant brain into wakefulness. Perry. *Hey, forget her,* a little voice whispered. *Why mess with this small stuff? Let's go get Macklin. Let's string him up by the balls before he starts his nonsense all over again. Do the world a favor.* I was appalled. Where had that come from? And why did I find that siren song so bloody attractive?

"Okay," I said quickly, unnerved by that whisper from the dark places of my heart. "I'll listen. But I'm not at my best in the middle of the night. Can this wait till tomorrow?"

"Well, all right. If you can meet me at six o'clock at my place, we can talk over breakfast. I have to be at work at seven-thirty, but we should have enough time."

"Okay," I yawned. "Where is your place?"

"On Beach Drive — the ocean side. Number

eighteen-eleven. It's white with a green door. Park in the driveway and walk through the gate to the back. I'll meet you there. And thanks, Caitlin."

I put the phone back in its cradle, scribbled the address down on a notepad, and fell back into the dark, warm pool of sleep.

CHAPTER FOUR
Wednesday

At quarter to six, more asleep than awake, I rolled into Perry's driveway. Sipping the last of my McDonald's morning coffee, I tossed the cup into my back seat trash bag, then stepped out into the chilly pre-dawn twilight of spring. I followed her directions to the back yard, except Perry's back yard was the ocean. A postage-stamp-sized lawn and some flowerbeds fell off abruptly to a twenty-foot wide stretch of rock and shingle beach. Beyond that lay the water. I squinted, shading my eyes, for the sun was just about to ease over the rim of the world.

"Caitlin!" called a female voice from the beach.

I walked down the flagstone path and peered over a six-foot drop. Below me, a woman rose from the waves. With the light behind her, she was a dark, mysterious figure — an alien being rising from an alien element. In one smooth motion, she raised her hands to wring the water from her hair, then began to walk toward me out of the ocean. All at once, goosebumps broke out all over my body. Whether it was the suddenness with which she had just *appeared* there in the water, or the fact that she seemed utterly at home in it, I was gripped by the beauty of this image. One part of me knew I was seeing only Perry in a wetsuit, but another part of me — the part of me that weeps when I read Hopkins' poetry, the part that gets chills every time I hear Judy Collins sing "The Great Silkie of Schule Skerry," the part that longs for beauty in a banal world — saw something else. I saw a strong woman having made herself one with courage, competence, and grace. I saw a warrior. And I felt joy. Edmund Spenser asked, in *The Faerie Queene:*

> Where is the antique glory now become
> That whilom wont in women to appear?

I knew that "antique glory" was here in front of me.

"Hi," I said to Perry, feeling distinctly insufficient. Triathlons? Ye Gods. Did she swim in the ocean *every* morning?

She ran up the flagstone steps, reaching behind

her to pull down the zipper of her blue wetsuit. "Great weather!" she exclaimed. "Don't you just love spring mornings?"

"Mmmm," I equivocated. I decided not to tell her that what I enjoyed most about spring mornings was lying in my bed just before the alarm went off, breathing the glorious scent of apple blossoms, and listening to the robins nest-building in the tree outside my window. Decidedly less vigorous pleasures. Attributable, no doubt, to my advancing age.

"Go on in through the side door," she said, pointing back along the path that led to the gate. "Make yourself comfortable. There's coffee brewed and bagels and cream cheese on the counter. And there's a bowl of fruit salad in the fridge. Help yourself. I need to get rid of this wetsuit and rinse off. I'll just be a minute."

I retraced my steps and found the kitchen door. Inside, I poured coffee and put a bagel in the toaster. The kitchen was painted yellow and white, and the sun poured in through the big windows, making everything glow. I took my bagel and coffee to the white-lacquered table in an alcove overlooking the ocean, and sat watching the water, waiting for Perry. In a few moments I heard sounds from somewhere in the house, and then she was in the kitchen behind me, humming. I turned to watch her. She was dressed in baggy pale blue sweats, and her hair, still damp, curled around her face in snaky blonde tendrils. She dished herself a bowl of fruit, poured coffee, and joined me at the table.

"Listen," she said, wasting no time, "I'm sorry for

acting like such a jerk. I ran off last night because I thought Tess would be in trouble. As it turned out, she wasn't, but I thought I'd better go see."

"Okay," I replied, mystified.

She took a few bites of bagel, chewing thoughtfully. "Like I told you last night, Tess's gone to live with a bunch of women out by Land's End."

"Crazy people, you said," I reminded her. "People who are all set to do something terrible."

She nodded. "Yeah."

"What?"

She put her bagel back on the plate and looked at me, blue eyes earnest. "Tess and I were yelling at each other when she told me this, so I may have it wrong. But I think it'll be a kind of . . . retaliation for the rapes. An incentive for the police to move their butts and catch the Full Moon Rapist." She grimaced. Evidently the memory of the yelling match was still painful. "Tess only let that slip because she was so angry with me for trying to track her down. She hung up on me. So that's all I know."

"Hmmm," I said. "Why should Tess and her friends care so much about this particular rapist?"

Perry shrugged.

"And you have no idea of what it is they plan to do? You told me last night you were afraid it would be something awful. Something that will probably send them to jail."

Perry made an impatient gesture. "I was only guessing. I said that because Tess bragged about how she wasn't afraid of going to jail for something she believed in."

"Oh? Like what?"

Perry shook her head. "I don't know. I'm sorry."

I sat back in my chair, feeling again that Perry was holding back, keeping something from me. It wasn't a good feeling.

"What I *do* know is that whatever they're going to do, they're going to do it soon," Perry offered. "Real soon."

How soon — the full moon? It seemed logical to me. Now I understood Perry's panic, her flight from the restaurant. "But the rapist struck ahead of schedule. Last night."

"Yeah," she nodded. "I guess it took them by surprise." Then she fell silent.

"Okay," I said when it looked as if she wasn't going to volunteer anything else. "Let's recap. You want me to get Tess away from these people before they do whatever it is they're gearing up to do. And I'll have to do it before the full moon, which is Friday." Fortunately, I'd looked it up in my almanac.

"Right."

"I charge two hundred and fifty dollars a day plus expenses. I need a thousand up front," I warned her, hoping my fee would put her off. My inner voice still whispered its blandishments, and I was having a hard time ignoring it.

"Oh. Well, my dad left me this house. His insurance paid off the mortgage, so all I have to worry about are the taxes and so on." She grimaced. "They're pretty awful — that's why I'm working part-time. But I do have money to pay you."

A question occurred to me. "Did Tess work too? You know — to help out?"

"No. I didn't want her to have the pressures I had. Our parents were killed in a car crash when I was twenty — five years ago. Tess was only

51

thirteen. So I kind of raised her. I think of her more as my kid than as my sister." Perry looked quickly away. "I was never a very good student anyway, so dropping out of my P.E. program at college was no big deal. Besides, I had to get a job to pay our expenses if we were going to stay here. I kind of dabbled around with triathlons — I was always a good athlete — till I saw that if I got serious about it I could make sports a career. My first pro competition is this weekend," she said. "There's a five-thousand-dollar first prize. Before this stuff started with Tess I really thought I could win. Now, I don't know. I haven't been sleeping well. I can't get up for training. Please," she begged. "This has to stop — for both our sakes."

"Tess's lucky to have someone who cares about her like you do," I remarked.

"She's the only family I have. Or am likely to have," she added cryptically.

"Are you paying Tess's college expenses too?"

Perry seemed about to say something, then changed her mind and just nodded.

I took a few sips of my coffee to give myself time to think over all this selflessness. At twenty, Perry had given up her college P.E. studies to raise Tess and keep this house. And send the kid to college. Now at twenty-five, just when she's launched her pro triathlon career, here's Tess again, needing something else. I'd be madder than hell at little sister. It wasn't Tess who needed help, I thought. Oh, she might be up to some idealistic silliness with her new friends, but I was willing to bet it was nothing serious. No, it was Perry who needed help. Perry needed a break from being superwoman. And from Tess. What did Tess need? As far as I could tell, Tess needed a damned good spanking.

"Before I make my decision, you need to know the ground rules. You have to be absolutely truthful with me," I reiterated. "You need to tell me everything. No lies by omission."

She nodded solemnly.

Damn it, why did I still feel uneasy? "I'll give you a report at the end, and a refund if I haven't spent all your money."

"That sounds all right."

"And you have to let me do things my way. I'll keep you informed, but I don't want any interference. I'm running the show."

She shrugged. "Okay."

"One more thing. Let's be realistic. If Tess genuinely wants to be with these people, all the persuasion in the world won't work. They evidently have something she needs. I'll try reason first, but she doesn't sound too amenable to reason."

"Try anything you like," Perry said. "Anything. Like you said, it's your show."

"Maybe the best I can do is just to get her away from them for this Friday. I doubt I can bring her back to you. She's not a runaway cat, after all."

Perry sighed. "That's all right. At least you'll have kept her out of trouble."

"Okay," I agreed.

"Okay? That's it?"

"Yeah. You're my employer now. You write me a check and I go to work. Maybe you can get your mind off Tess for a while and go swim or whatever it is you need to do to get ready for that competition."

"I have to bike forty miles," she told me. "Right after work. It's my weakest event and I really have to concentrate on it." She looked at me, a curious expression in her eyes. "Being a private eye, what's it like?"

I lifted an eyebrow and decided to tell her half the truth. "It's just my business. I'm not an angel of mercy, Perry. It's a job. Something I've found I do well. And there seems to be a demand for my services."

"Oh," she said, sounding disappointed. Evidently she wanted more. Tough luck. She was buying my services, not my soul. And although I admired Perry, something about her bothered me. I couldn't put my finger on it, but something seemed wrong. She had become too submissive, too compliant.

"Here are some things I need," I told her, scribbling a list on a notepad I dug out of my jacket pocket. "Addresses and phone numbers of Tess's friends, her courses at U Vic, a current picture. That kind of thing. It'll probably take you a while to get it all together. Give me a call when it's ready and I'll come get it."

She looked over the list. "Okay. Later on this evening I should have it all. But here's something you can get started on." She took a scratch pad from a little table by the window. "Tess's best friend, Julia Springer. At least they were best friends until Tess got into this mess."

She walked me to the kitchen door. "I'm glad I called you," she said. "I know you can help. And, like I said, I'm sorry I acted like such a jerk. It won't happen again."

"Hey, it's allowed, you know," I told her.

She shook her head. Evidently triathletes weren't permitted a single moment of funk. "No," she said firmly. Whether she was trying to convince me or herself, I wasn't sure.

"Go drive your truck," I told her, wishing I could like her a little more. "I'll talk to you later."

The address Perry had given me for Julia Springer was in the old, monied section of Victoria called Uplands. In that ever-so-exclusive enclave of the super rich, the lawns are lush, soccer-field sized, and so green they hurt your eyes. And they're absolutely weedless. Monstrous oaks, overgrown rhododendrons, and mutant azaleas conspire to hide the houses from the impious gazes of us commoners; however, here and there a wayward gable peeks out from under cover. The Springer property sprawled across a park-like acre of emerald turf, and it took me a full three minutes of cruising back and forth to locate the driveway. I parked my MG behind a brand new silver Corvette whose vanity plates read 4 JOOL then tried, unsuccessfully, to saunter along the gravel path and up the white marble steps as though I did this every day. I rang the bell, expecting to be told that deliveries were made around back.

After only a few moments of waiting, the door was opened by a young woman in gray cords and a red wool sweater, a faded denim jacket over one arm. Her long, shiny brown hair was tied back with a maroon paisley silk scarf and she had a set of car keys in her hand.

"Julia Springer?" I guessed.

She was clearly surprised. "Yes. Who are you?" She had pretty brown eyes and a small, straight nose covered with freckles.

"Caitlin Reece." I held out my hand and she took it. "I'm looking for Tess Eldon. Her sister told me you two were friends."

Amazingly, her lower lip started to tremble, and when she glanced at me, a whole volume of betrayal and hurt could be read there. Then, clearly angry with herself for this moment of weakness, she brushed tears from her eyes with the back of her hand.

"I'd like to talk to you if you have the time," I pressed. "Why don't we go somewhere and have breakfast? Or coffee?"

She was plainly skeptical. "Can you really find her? The last time I saw her — when she went home to get some clothes — she wouldn't even talk to me, and I'm her best friend." She hung her head. "Was her best friend."

I shrugged. "Can I find her? Probably." She looked doubtful. "Hey, this is an island," I said. "There are only so many places to hide." She nodded, wanting to believe. "And Perry's told me she's holed up near Land's End somewhere." She looked at me, waiting for more. "As for persuading her to come home, well, I'll give it my best shot. But in order to do that, I need to know what made her run off to Land's End in the first place. Perry says she doesn't know."

Julia made a face.

"Yeah, that's what I think, too. Well, what about it? Will you help me?"

She thought this over for a few long moments. "All right," she said finally. "Where will we go?"

"How about The Blethering Place? On Oak Bay Avenue. Shall I meet you there or do you want to come with me?"

She looked down the driveway to where my MG was parked. I was acutely aware of the red primer paint on the front right-hand bumper, the ding in the door.

For a kid, she was amazingly tactful. "Why don't I meet you there," she said smoothly. "I have some errands to run later."

"Sure," I replied as we walked together to 4 JOOL. I left her there, poor little rich kid climbing into her fancy car. But as hard as I tried, I couldn't feel sorry for her. Money might not buy happiness, but given the choice, I'd rather be rich and miserable than poor and miserable. Who wouldn't?

I resisted ordering one of the humongous cheese scones The Blethering Place is famous for. Instead, I sent the waitress for coffee as I waited for Julia. With its wood-beamed ceilings, its collection of almost-antique furniture, its teapots with their eccentric, hand-knitted tea cozies, and its general air of Olde England, The Blethering Place is a favorite tourist stop. Fortunately March was too early for tourists, so we locals had the place to ourselves.

Julia found a parking place for the Corvette right out front and came bouncing into the tea shop. Youth, good nutrition, and good genes made her fairly glow. She saw me, waved, and came on over.

"I'll have a cheese scone," she told the waitress. "And tea. Oh, could you bring some honey, please?"

I sipped my coffee and tried to ignore the pleading of my stomach. *Lunch. We'll have lunch soon. No snacks,* I told it.

"Are you a student at U Vic?" I asked while she drenched her scone with honey and poured tea.

She nodded. "Political science. Tess was in all my classes until this term. Then she started taking weird things."

"Weird things?"

"You know, all that fringy stuff. Courses in women's studies. Feminism. That kind of thing."

I tried not to smile. "Tonia Konig's courses?"

"Yeah. And Diana McNeil's, too. Women's mysteries or heroine's journeys or some such thing."

"And you weren't interested?"

She gave me a frosty look. "I'm a student of politics. International relations. I'm not a feminist. I have no axe to grind."

I couldn't let that one go by. "Isn't the study of politics the study of power? Who has it, or had it, how they lost it, how someone else got it."

"Well, you could put it that way," she agreed reluctantly. "So what?"

"So lots. Women are the most disenfranchised group in the world. The most powerless. They make ten percent of the world's money and own one percent of the world's property. How can you ignore that if you're studying power?"

"I can ignore that because I choose to," she informed me. "I don't want all that stuff warping my mind. Making me shrill and antagonistic."

That set me back on my heels. "The way it did Tess?"

"Evidently," she said, still frosty. "It was McNeil's class that put all those *feminist* ideas into her head."

"Like what?"

Her nostrils flared a little. "You said it yourself. Power. Why women don't have any. And how they can get it."

I was interested. "Oh? How?"

She sighed. "By doing dumb things. Taking inner journeys. Identifying with the feminine. Rejecting the masculine. Making your own myths. Flaky stuff. Not scholarship."

I smiled a little. "If it hasn't been written by dead German men, then it isn't any good, is that it?"

She blushed to the roots of her hair. "I didn't say that." She sneaked a glance at me, saw my raised eyebrow and amended her statement. "Well, not exactly. But, listen. If you don't *know* any history or any political theory — all that stuff written by dead German men — how can you even begin to put the new stuff into context? To make any sense of it?"

"That seems reasonable," I admitted. "As long as you keep an open mind about all the flaky stuff."

She blushed again. "Okay, I know I sound intolerant. It's just that Tess threw herself into all that pseudo scholarship. All that New Age writing. It was as though it . . ." She shook her head, clearly at a loss for words.

"Filled a void?" I guessed. "Answered a need?"

"Yeah," she nodded. "She said that until she took Diana McNeil's courses, she hadn't realized that she had gone through life half-asleep." She shrugged. "*I* think it's silly."

"Tess didn't."

"I know," she whispered, hurt in her voice. "Why didn't she, though? We were . . . like sisters. Closer than sisters. We've been friends since grade school. I thought I knew her better than anyone in the world. How could there be a part of her that I didn't know, a part of her that," she sniffled, making no effort to hide the tears now, "that needed all *that?* And how could it become more important than anything we shared?"

I handed her a napkin and she dabbed and blew. Quite a speech. Closer than sisters, eh? I wondered just how close that was and tried not to jump to the obvious conclusion.

"Sorry," she said.

"It's okay. So, after she took Diana McNeil's courses, then what?"

"Well, she joined a study group. Some of the women from McNeil's classes used to meet to discuss ideas in her books. They invited Tess to join them. I think they met a couple times a week. Then a funny thing happened."

I waited.

"Tess said they asked her to come and live with them. I remember how excited she was. She explained to me that they didn't ask just anybody. They told her she needed to live with them so they could support her in her spiritual journey." She pursed her lips.

"And that's when Tess left home?"

"Right."

"Julia, did Tess ever say anything about this study group wanting money from her?"

Her eyes got wide. "You mean like the Moonies?"

"Yeah."

She thought. "No. But Tess didn't have much money anyhow. Well, that's not true. She has her trust fund."

"Her trust fund?"

"Yeah. Her dad set some money aside for her. Quite a lot, I think. She gets a quarter of it when she turns eighteen, a quarter when she turns twenty-one, and the other half at twenty-five."

A trust fund! Why hadn't Perry told me? Then I thought of something. "Julia, Perry said Tess just turned eighteen."

"She did? Oh God, that's right. Just after Valentine's Day. I should have remembered." She looked stricken.

"What was this trust fund worth — do you know?"

"A couple hundred thousand in all. I think Tess was to get, like, fifty thousand when she turned eighteen."

No wonder Tess's study group wanted her to come and live with them. Fifty grand would buy a nifty spiritual journey. I wondered how they had found out about it.

"Poor Tess," Julia said. "They didn't want her at all. They wanted her money."

"Poor Tess," I agreed. "Listen, I have two more questions for you about the trust fund. I need you to think carefully, okay?"

She nodded.

"Did Tess tell you whether Perry had a similar fund?"

She shook her head. "No. Their dad left Perry the house and Tess a trust fund. They both knew that."

Very interesting indeed. "You don't happen to know who Tess's trustees are, do you?"

"Sure. Gelven, Reilly, and Telford. They have offices on Government Street. Tess used to joke about them. The keepers of the loot, she called them."

I sat back, thoughtful. This put a whole different light on things. I couldn't wait to discuss it with the elder Miss Eldon.

"When did you and Tess stop talking to each other?"

"I never stopped talking to her," Julia said. "But she stopped talking to me, oh, right after the Christmas break. Sometime early in January. We'd been out on a date with two guys from the basketball team. That was Saturday. Monday was the first day of the new term, and when Tess didn't show up for the classes we were taking together, I stopped by her house to see if she was sick or something."

"Was she?"

"No. She wasn't even there. I called that night, and Perry said she was out. I didn't catch up with her until Friday, and by that time, she had changed her whole schedule. She was taking two of Diana McNeil's classes, a sociology class, and something in women's studies."

"Quite a change."

"For Tess, yeah, it was. She always seemed so . . . sure of herself. Like she knew exactly where she was going."

"Where was that?"

"She was going to be a U.N. interpreter. She was studying languages and taking classes in politics. She started studying Russian when she was in high school — we both did, but she kept it up. She's a lot smarter than me," Julia admitted ruefully. "And she began studying Japanese and Chinese." She glared at me indignantly. "But she lost interest in all of that."

I signaled the waitress for more coffee for me and more hot water for Julia and drummed my fingers on the tabletop.

"Do you know what the study group does?" I inquired tactfully. "Apart from discussing ideas in Diana McNeil's books."

"What do you mean?"

"You said they wanted to help Tess take a spiritual journey. What do you think that involves?"

She bit her lip. "I don't know. Tess wouldn't tell me. I know they're into women's rights, though — they give speeches and write letters to the campus paper. They belong to some weird-sounding group, but I can't remember the name. Sorry."

I thought about the women I had met on campus the other night. A memory tried to surface — something triggered by our meeting — and I tabled it for later consideration.

"You know," she continued, "the day I found Tess at home, packing, the last time I saw her, I begged her to tell me what was going on, what she was doing. I told her I cared about her, that I wanted to understand. But she wouldn't say a word. And she looked so . . . different."

"Different how?"

"Well, Tess always took such pride in her appearance. She didn't have a whole lot of money, but she bought nice clothes. When I saw her, though, she was dressed in dirty jeans, a flannel shirt, and work boots. She hadn't washed her hair lately and she even had dirt under her fingernails!"

I pulled out my notebook and gave it and a pen to Julia. "Would you write down the names of those courses Tess took, anyone you can recall who might have been in her classes, and anyone you know in that study group. Oh, and any boyfriends, too."

She looked quickly away. "Tess didn't have a boyfriend."

"I thought you said the two of you went out with some basketball players."

"Uh huh. But that was the only time. They were just a couple of frat guys who had been pestering us for dates."

"Still, let me have their names, okay?" I sipped my coffee. "Do you have a boyfriend, Julia?"

She shook her head, still avoiding my eyes, and I decided not to push it. I'd get answers to everything in time.

Julia bent over the notebook, scribbling briskly. When she gave it back to me, there were four names on it as well as the titles of Diana McNeil's courses.

"Okay," I said, pocketing the notebook. "Thanks. This has been a big help." I fished some money out of my pocket to pay the bill and rose to leave. Julia walked with me to the door. Outside, on the sidewalk, we squinted in the pale light. The sun, after its early morning effulgence, had decided not to grace us with its presence. Instead it had hidden somewhere behind a sky the color of opals. From the roof of one of the little shops, a robin peeped dispiritedly. Clearly he, too, had expected better things.

"Miss Reece, I know you're not working for me," Julia said awkwardly, "but could you, you know, let me know what happens?"

I smiled. "I might be able to do better than that. When I find her, maybe you'd like to come along with me to talk to her."

Julia's face lit up. "Oh, I would," she said. "I really would. But will she even see me?"

"Maybe," I told her, trying to sound confident. "Friends don't usually turn their backs on each other and walk away. I think she'll see you." And Perry, too, I vowed. You don't just kiss off the people who care about you. "I can't guarantee what will happen afterwards, though."

"Thank you," she said, eyes shining with tears. "You know, Tess and I . . ." She trailed off, and giving me a last, haunted look, ran for the safety of 4 JOOL.

CHAPTER FIVE

The feeling that Tess needed a damned good spanking and that Perry needed to write out the definition of honesty one hundred times intensified as I drove to U Vic. I parked in the lot I had parked in last night and began to walk the short distance to Nootka Hall. I was angry with Tess and Perry, I realized, but my anger was bigger than it should have been. I was furious and I wondered if this wasn't my ego's way of distracting me from the voice that urged me to put this case aside and go after Macklin with a straight razor. I'd have to keep that anger under control. Practice some self-restraint. Composure. Feigning that elusive emotion, I mounted the steps of Nootka Hall and went in search of Tonia Konig.

I found her in her office, reading student papers, or at least looking at the words. Her dark hair shone, and I knew that when she looked up, the smoky blue of her eyes would match exactly the blue cashmere pullover she wore. I knew, too, that her pants would be navy blue wool, and that somewhere would be a matching navy blue lambskin jacket. And although I knew these things about Tonia Konig — what colors she liked to wear, what she drank, what scent she used — in many of the important ways I knew nothing at all. Tonia had been one-half of my employer team a couple of years ago. She had thought me a thug; I had thought her a snotty academic wimp, albeit a very attractive wimp. We came to an accord in bed — a liaison that was, to say the least, unlikely. But now we had an unscaleable wall lying between us — the body of the man she had killed one spring night. The man she had killed to save me. And until that wall fell, we could never be anything to each other. That had been over two years ago, and although I had often wanted to, I had never picked up the phone to call her. Some part of me knew that the call had to come from her. It never had.

"Any pearls of wisdom there?" I inquired from the doorway.

"Oh, not many," she said, looking at me over the tops of her glasses and smiling. "So what brings you to the halls of academe?"

I smiled uneasily. "Oh, you know. Woman's

endless quest for knowledge. Answers to the eternal questions. Contemplation of the immutable verities."

"Such as?"

"Wanna have lunch?"

She grinned, took off her glasses, and squared up the pile of papers in front of her. "Best offer I've had all morning."

"Tell me about Diana McNeil," I asked her, once the waiter had deposited a couple of Labatt's Blues on the table.

"Diana McNeil — what on earth do you want to know about her for?" Tonia asked in amazement.

"Tess Eldon is missing," I told her. "Her best friend thinks something she learned in one of Diana's courses had a big influence on her."

Tonia took a swallow of her beer, her head thrown back, the muscles of her strong pale throat working. She put down the glass, and as she did, she glanced at me quickly and caught me looking at her. I didn't look away. Neither did she.

"Diana McNeil," she said, after a moment. "Well, she's only been on the U Vic faculty since September. Came from a college on the mainland, I think. She's one of those rare creatures: she has a solid academic reputation but at the same time is pretty well-known in the popular press. Or so it's rumored."

"Rumored? You mean you don't know?"

She shook her head, the glossy hair moving with her. "No. I do little enough reading in my own field. Maybe I'm getting old, but those student papers seem to take up more of my time every year. And they're not getting any better," she groused.

The waiter brought our salads, twirled the pepper mill around, and disappeared. I stabbed a coin of zucchini and in between bites continued my questions. "So what does she teach?"

"Two classes. She's only a part-time faculty member. Let's see, the courses are listed in women's studies — 'Women's Mysteries' and 'The Heroine's Journey.' I'm not sure."

"They sound interesting, but a little soft-headed."

"Tut, tut," Tonia admonished me. "The students say she's a good teacher and her classes are always over-subscribed."

"Yeah, but what do nineteen-year-olds know, anyhow?"

"True."

We nibbled companionably for a few moments. "What do you know about Diana herself?"

Tonia took another swallow of beer and licked a bit of foam off her upper lip with the tip of her tongue. "Well, her lover was murdered last year. Diana took it very hard. Rumor has it that she spent some time in a high-priced institution." Tonia shrugged. "She certainly never talks about her past."

"Was the lover male or female?"

"Female. Why? Does it matter?"

"It might."

Tonia finished the last of her salad. "You know, you might talk to Marge Sherman about Diana. Marge owns Concordia Books. Diana read there during the Christmas break. The place was packed, so the students tell me. I intended to go, but something came up."

She looked at me and smiled her megawatt smile and my toes curled inside my Reeboks. Tonia never had any idea of the effect she had on me. Sadly, I realized I had never had the opportunity to tell her.

I cleared my throat and with some difficulty continued, "Are Marge and Diana friends?"

Tonia shook her head. "More like good acquaintances." After a moment's silence, she asked, a little too brightly. "Caitlin, what are you doing Saturday night?"

I hardly knew what to say. "I have no idea what I'll be doing Saturday," I told her truthfully. "I've just started working on a new case. Sometimes these things develop pretty fast." To my amazement, Tonia actually looked disappointed. "But sometimes they don't. Why? What did you have in mind?" Was this what it seemed to be? A rekindling of an old attraction? I tried my best to sound nonchalant. After all, she could be feeling me out to dog-sit.

"I was wondering . . . would you like to come over to Vancouver with me? There's a great comic appearing at the Women's Club. We can have dinner and laugh a little. What do you say?"

I was so surprised, I just stared. Tonia Konig was asking me out. Another woman was asking *me* out. That hadn't happened for, oh, fifteen years. You see, usually *I* do the asking. Egads, was this a Real Date? Or were we to be just two old warhorses doing the town together? "I, um, well, thank you. Yes, I'd love to come." Oh, that sounded swell. "If I'm not tied up, that is."

She raised an eyebrow. "That might be fun."

"With my new case," I told her sternly.

"Ah yes, the new case."

"Why don't I give you a call Saturday morning?" I said. "I should have a pretty good feel then for how things are going."

"Okay."

We left some money on the table and walked out of the restaurant to the street where our cars were parked. She was walking just a little ahead and suddenly, as if having come to an abrupt decision, she turned to face me. Out here in the light of day I was reminded all over again of how truly beautiful Tonia Konig was — flawless complexion; dark, glossy hair cut just below her ears; even, white teeth; and those indigo eyes.

"You know, I always meant to call you after we . . . after that Buchanan thing."

No reply seemed called for, so I just waited.

"I had a hard time for a while," she went on. "Squaring my beliefs with the fact that I *killed* someone." Reluctant to meet my eyes, she looked at a point somewhere over my left shoulder. "I wanted to call you and talk to you about it. But the more I thought about it, the more I became convinced that you wouldn't . . . that you might not . . ." She moved her shoulders in what might have been a shrug. "I guess I don't know what I'm trying to say."

I thought I knew. "C'mon," I said, taking her arm. "Let's walk."

We crossed the cobbled street and walked in silence down to the seawall below the stately Empress Hotel. An Air BC float plane was just coming in for a landing in the harbor, its pontoons kicking up two white plumes of spray.

"When I first went into business for myself, I had to kill someone," I told Tonia. "A young guy. He was just twenty-one. He had kidnapped a little girl — a neighbor's ten-year-old — and her mom hired me to get her back. Well, I tracked them down to a decrepit old motel just outside Parksville. He and his buddy had the little girl pretty well doped. They intended to hole up there for a day or two and then take her to their fishing shack on one of the islands. She'd been there for three days when I found them. The buddy was off buying beer when I broke in. The young guy grabbed a gun and put it to the little girl's head. I remember his exact words: 'It's loaded,' he said. 'I'll blow her brains out before I let you take me. Back off, bitch. Put the gun on the floor and back off.' I had come in the window with my .357 drawn, but he had the drop on me. What could I do? I had just about decided to back off and call in the cops when a voice in my head told me that he intended to do it anyway. To blow her brains out. Right after he blew out mine. He didn't have a thing to lose." I squinted out across the pewter-colored bay.

"What did you do?" Tonia whispered.

"I shot the bastard in the head."

I turned to face her and told her something I've never told anyone else. "I didn't spend one instant thinking of being merciful. Wondering about the right thing to do. Because I don't think we have the luxury to be merciful in the presence of evil. Instead, I think we have an obligation. I don't think evil can be unmade. So I think we have to stop it. However we can. I think we have to stand between it and what it wants." I shrugged. "I try not to worry too much about the fact that I had to kill him. I try to concentrate instead on the gift I gave the little girl."

"The gift?"

"Her life, Tonia. I gave her her life. Just the way you gave me mine." Her eyes were pools of lapis lazuli. I could have fallen in and drowned, but I had something else to say. "I've never thanked you for it, either, but it isn't the sort of event you commemorate with a Hallmark card."

"What about the little girl?" Tonia asked.

"She's in high school now. Her mom writes me a letter every Christmas. She's had a lot of therapy. People care about her. She'll be okay." I reached over and brushed a strand of hair off her cheek. "What about you?"

She shivered and looked away. "I had trouble sleeping at first," she said. "And I still have bad dreams. But to have done otherwise, to have let that *creature* kill you —" She bit her lip.

"You thought I wouldn't understand," I told her. "That I would be impatient with you. After all, you started out thinking I was a thug."

She nodded, eyes downcast, ashamed. "I should have known better."

"I waited for you to call. I didn't want to push you. I wanted you to want to talk to me."

She looked up at me and, taking her hands out of her pockets, raised one finger to my lips. I couldn't help myself. I kissed it.

"I have," she whispered. "I will. Thank you for letting me start."

We walked in silence back to our cars.

CHAPTER SIX

There's at least one thing that can be said about life — it's never boring. I contemplated this puerile insight all the way back to my house. I had gone to see Tonia for information. Well, I had surely gotten it. Life was full of surprises.

Indeed it was. In my study, the computer was on again. This time the pithy amber message was:

87p[;;; 87 rttttr yuh yuh] 543eesteeee k

"Aargh!" I yelled. "That's it! Absolutely it! Spawn of the devil, you're going back to your maker. I refuse to live with something I can't figure out." I punched its power button, killing the message instantly. Feeling like a Neanderthal, I stomped into the kitchen, looking for something I *could* understand. My cats, for instance. The phone interrupted my search.

"Caitlin, I'm so glad you're there! I've been calling and calling."

It was Wendy Murdoch. My heartbeat about doubled. "What's up?"

"It's Pansy. I was so scared the other night, I forgot about her. Caitlin, I left her behind."

"Who?"

"Pansy. My cat!"

"Your cat. Of course," I said dumbly. In my mind I saw the little wicker cat bed on the front porch.

"Do you think it would be all right if I went back for her? After work?"

"Definitely and absolutely not," I said. "Can't you call a neighbor to grab her for you?"

"Well, she's kind of unpredictable," Wendy said apologetically. "When she was a kitten she was thrown out of a car onto my front lawn, and she's never gotten over that. She only lets certain people near her. Caitlin, I'm afraid of what Macklin might do to her. Can you think of something?"

"Sure," I said, resigned. After all, hadn't I promised I'd help? I'd snatched her from the fangs and claws of Macklin. How hard could it be to similarly snatch a cat? "I'll get her for you. Don't worry."

"How?"

"I have a friend who's good with animals," I said, projecting cheer. "She'll know what to do."

"Well, okay." She sounded distinctly doubtful.

"Say, did you contact the police?"

"Uh huh. They went out to the house, too. They didn't seem very concerned, though. They thought it could just be a prank."

I ground my teeth. Maybe I'd have Sandy talk to them. "What are you planning to do?"

"Well, I'm still talking things over with Viv and the others. I might move in here with them. Although they have some friends they say I can stay with if I'd rather. But I'm definitely going to move. Listen, I gotta get back to work. Will you call me about Pansy?"

"Sure I will. I'll get her. She'll be fine. Don't worry." Ha. Famous last words.

"Patience," Gray Ng told me. "You need patience to catch a feral cat. And love."

"Yeah, but patience and love take time. I don't have time. I have to do my catnapping this afternoon. Snatch and grab."

She looked at me inscrutably. "When time is short, try tuna."

"What's that, a Confucian saying?" I was not amused.

"Certainly not. It's practical advice. Try tuna. And a humane trap."

Gray Ng and I stood in the meadow outside her small cedar-shingled house in the woods. A sign on the highway directed prospective clients to Gray's animal psychology practice which could be reached by driving down a quarter mile of wooded lane. Today she was busy leading a pretty bay horse around a pocket-sized meadow while I tagged at their heels. She stopped and tied him to a tree. The bay dropped his head and nuzzled the ground, looking for a grassy snack.

"Perplexing," she admitted, hands in the pockets of her tan down vest. "But he will tell me about it in his own time." Gray came up to about my shoulder, and dressed as she was in an old white sweatshirt and jeans, jet black hair cropped short, she looked about fourteen. Until you saw her eyes. Then you knew different. A Vietnamese emigre, one of the Boat People, Gray had said very little to me about her past, and I had never pried.

What I did know about her was that she could understand animals — really understand them. Vets referred their clients' problem pets to her, and she now had all the business she could handle. Not bad for someone who was fired from her job as a veterinary assistant for being a "damned Asian witch."

Her two constant companions, a pair of brindled Great Danes she called The Girls, snoozed close by. Their master had brought them to the vet where Gray was working and requested their euthanization. They were unmanageable, he said. According to the story I got from one of Gray's former co-workers, Gray had gone around back to where the ferocious duo was penned and looked at them for a long time. Then she said something to them in Vietnamese and opened the kennel door. They came out smiling doggy smiles, tails wagging, bellies on the ground, dying to lick her hands. Gray and the Great Danes were sent packing together that same day.

"So what's he here for?" I inquired of the horse.

"He won't allow himself to be tied to posts," Gray told me.

"But he's tied now."

She looked at me reprovingly. "This is a tree, Caitlin. An alder. Not a post."

"Oh."

"Come around back," she said. "I can give you a trap. The rest you must provide yourself."

"Yeah, I guess I can handle that."

She patted my arm. "I have every confidence you can."

Too many hours later, armed with a can of Nine Lives tuna, a can opener, and a humane trap, I drove into Saanich. What with one thing and another I had frittered away the whole afternoon. It was now almost seven o'clock, and dusk. I ground my teeth in frustration. I had wanted to be here much earlier. How was I going to even spot the elusive Pansy in the dark? For that matter, what did the cat look like? Belatedly, I realized I hadn't asked. Great. Just great. How would I be able to tell her from all the other neighborhood freeloaders? Once they got a whiff of tuna, I was sure every cat on the island would put in an appearance.

I decided to try to do things the easy way. Parking my MG in Wendy's driveway, I walked out to the road and up the sidewalk of seven fifty-three

Lochside. The house was dark, but I pounded on the door anyhow. No luck. With a sigh I walked over to seven fifty-five. There, lights were on and, in response to my vigorous and persistent knocking, the door opened. An ancient wrinkled woman, white hair in a frizz around her head, one thin, birdlike hand clutching her bathrobe, stood there regarding me with eyes like little black buttons. I had uttered barely two words when she cupped a hand behind her ear and yelled, "Eh?"

I've had these conversations before — usually they degenerate into unproductive shouting matches. I didn't feel like shouting tonight. Whipping out my notebook I wrote HAVE YOU SEEN THE NEIGHBOR'S CAT? on a piece of paper and shoved it under her nose.

The ancient looked at the note as if it were the Rosetta Stone, fingered it, smiled a toothless smile, and closed the door in my face. Wonderful. I have such a deft touch.

"Okay Pansy," I muttered to myself. "It's just you and me."

Schlepping my load through a break in Wendy's cedar hedge and around the side of the house, I debated the manner in which to announce my arrival. What would be most efficacious, I wondered, an ambiguous "Kitty, kitty, kitty," or a more straightforward "Num nums for Pansy?" Phooey. If I were a cat, I wouldn't twitch a whisker for either one.

I put the trap down on the grass, knelt beside it, opened the tuna, and placed it just behind the trigger plate. Then I loaded the trap. I was just brushing off my hands when I heard a noise from the back yard. A kind of rhythmic huffing noise, like the sound a runner might make at the end of a quick and hilly five miles. I rose to my feet, drew my .357, and peered around the corner of the house. A slight, dark-haired figure in a hooded sweatshirt and jeans held a white cat out at arm's length by its collar, a hammer in his free hand. The huffing sound was coming from the cat, who was strangling.

I took three running steps forward and kicked the son of a bitch just behind one knee. He let out a yelp of pain and surprise and fell on his face. The cat hit the ground beside him, drew in one noisy *aoooof* of air, and took off. I fell on top of the prostrate figure, knees first, grabbed a handful of hair, and pulled his head back. Then I rammed the barrel of my .357 as far as it would go into his right ear. Sean Macklin's ear.

"Hey!" he sobbed. "Are you nuts? You're hurting me! Let go!"

"Shut up," I hissed, hitching myself off him and yanking him to his knees. "Put your hands on top of your head, you little shit."

"What is this?" he demanded. "A shakedown? Are you a cop? I'm clean. You can search me if you want to."

"I wouldn't want to get my hands dirty," I told him. By now I was shaking with rage. To my horror I heard myself cock the hammer of my revolver. Macklin heard it, too, and he began to blubber.

"What do you *want*? Money? I've got about thirty bucks in my wallet. That's all. Take it. Hey, man, just tell me what this is all *about*. Whatever it is, whatever you want, I'll do it."

My hand seemed to belong to someone else. As if in a dream, I saw the hand's thumb on the hammer, the index finger moving to begin the trigger pull. And as I watched, I felt a dark, gleeful bubble build up inside me, a silent black laugh, and heard a voice yammering: *Kill him pull the trigger blow the little bastard's brains out his other ear he deserves it do the world a favor shoot the son of a bitch no one will ever know shoot him shoot him shoot himmmmmmmmm.*

Appalled, panicked, I prayed for the strength not to pull the trigger. As I did so, there was a high humming sound in my head that made me dizzy. I closed my eyes for an instant and when I opened them, the humming was gone. So was the voice. My hand and my will were my own again. I very carefully removed the .357 from Macklin's ear and eased the hammer off. I felt suddenly very tired.

"Oh, thank you," he blubbered. "Thank you. I'll give you anything you want, anything —"

"Shut your mouth, Macklin," I told him wearily. I stood up and backed several steps away from him. "Get up and turn around and look at me."

He scrambled a little, got his feet under him, and came up swinging the hammer he had been clutching all along. The swing missed me by about a yard and before he had a chance to wind up for another one I moved in and kicked him — in the kneecap of the leg I had kicked earlier. He howled this time and, dropping the hammer, fell to the ground, both hands clasped around his knee. I let him cry for about ten seconds.

"Stop pissing and moaning and pay attention," I

told him. To my gratification, he shut up. "I'm only going to tell you this once. Stay away from here. Away. Read my lips, asshole: A-W-A-Y. Away. Away from Wendy Murdoch, her cat, her house, and everything else associated with her. Got it?"

He snuffled, half sat up, and raised his head, a hound on a promising scent. "Who are you? How do you know me?" His teary eyes focused. "A broad? You're a broad?" he croaked in disbelief.

"I believe the correct noun is 'woman,' and yes, I most definitely am. And when you're limping to work tomorrow, I hope you'll remember that it was a woman who whipped your sorry ass. We're not all defenseless, Macklin. And believe me, if I see you anywhere near here, I'll do it all over again."

"I know you," he said suddenly, and despite my tough talk, a little finger of fear touched the back of my neck. "Who the hell are you?"

"Never mind. Just get up and get out of here."

He rolled cautiously to his feet, eyeing my gun. I knew what he was thinking.

"Forget it," I said. "You're not half fast enough."

He looked from the gun to my face and something he saw there must have convinced him to be prudent. He opened his mouth to deliver some parting tough-guy threats, but I wasn't in the mood for chest-beating.

"Just bugger off," I told him. "And remember what I said. Don't come back."

Wiping his nose on the sleeve of his sweatshirt, he hobbled off into the darkness.

* * * * *

82

It was well after midnight when Pansy finally put in an appearance. I had driven twice to the Driftwood Drift-In for coffee and the restroom. Cold, angry, and depressed, I was sitting in my MG in Wendy's driveway, when a little white cat came through the cedar hedge. As she circled the trap warily, I saw that she wasn't completely white — one ear, her tail, one back leg, and a spot on her chest were a darker color. Maybe fawn or apricot.

"C'mon Pansy baby," I breathed, "get on in there." Just then, a dog bayed somewhere down the street and she shied violently, crouched low, ready to run. A fat flotilla of clouds sailed across the face of the moon, and when I could see again, Pansy was gone.

"Well, that's that," I said aloud in disgust. Try tuna indeed. I walked stiffly over to the trap, released the trigger, and loaded the trap back into my car. Taking a can of tuna over to the porch, I deposited it next to the cat bed and pushed them both a little farther under the roof overhang. In case of rain. Then I fluffed the pillow. "Tomorrow," I promised Wendy. "I'll try again tomorrow."

I lay in bed with a glass of Scotch, cats curled at my feet, and thought about Macklin. Shit. If only that phone gizmo had been capable of yielding prints. Bad luck. Well, why not try to find out the terms of his parole? His little stunt with Pansy might well have been enough to land him back in jail. I knew his parole information would be buried somewhere at Metro, along with the trial and sentencing proceedings, and although Sandy could eventually dig it out, I knew someone who could dig faster.

Francis the Ferret answered his phone on the second ring, *mirabile dictu*. But then I remembered — Francis was awake when the rest of the world was asleep. I wasn't sure about vice versa, though. I suspected he just folded himself up like a vampire bat and hung by his toenails in the coat closet for a while, chuckling in the dark.

"Caitlin," he said cheerily. "What can five hundred dollars do for you?"

"You've always had such a way with words," I told him testily, "but here's something even you might not be able to handle."

"Oh really? What?" I sensed interest. Francis loves a professional challenge.

"The computer at the prison. I want to see someone's file. His psych profile, too. And I also want to look at the terms of his parole — you know, what he has to do to land back inside. Think you can take a peek for me?"

"Oooh," he said with a delighted little squeal. "I don't believe we've been to prison before." The "we" in question was he and his computer, of course. Francis never goes anywhere — he lets his fingers do the walking. And as far as I know, they've walked into just about every major database in the country. Electronic breaking and entering is his specialty. He assures his customers that there is no database anywhere that is safe from his fiddling, and I have no reason to doubt him. He's come through for me time and time again. Francis is an expensive little bloodsucker, but a very competent one. "We'll have to buy some passwords — that's a so-called secure system — so it'll cost you more. But I don't believe there'll be any serious problem. Give me a name, dearie, and I'll get started."

"Macklin. Sean Macklin."

"Got it."

"I'll bring the money by your mail drop tomorrow."

"Today, you mean."

"Oh yeah, today. 'Time's winged chariot' and all that."

"If I'm not being too bold, you seem a little distracted, sweetling. Dispirited, too."

"Yes to both observations."

"I don't want to sound crass, but if the information you want will improve your mood, I could rush."

"For an extra two-fifty, you mean."

"Of course. Everything costs."

Tell me about it. "No thanks. I'll take your regular service."

"Whatever," he said blithely.

"Night, Francis."

He hung up, humming.

I scrunched a little lower in bed, took another swallow of my Scotch, and stroked a cat with my foot. With Francis' help I might just be able to give Mr. Macklin enough rope to hang himself. I certainly didn't want to repeat the scene in Wendy's backyard. No thank you. Because I wasn't sure I'd have the strength to resist shooting him. And that was the cause of my distraction and dispiritedness. Under fire, as it were, I had failed to measure up to my image of myself. When I replayed the scene in my mind where I had cocked my .357's hammer, I felt physically ill. And I felt sicker when I allowed myself to experience that emotion again — a dark, devouring, gleeful avidity. I was going to kill him and I was going to enjoy killing him. I lusted for Macklin's death. *But you didn't kill him,* a sensible voice said inside my head. *You put the gun down.*

I swallowed the last of my Scotch, punched my pillow into shape, and pulled my comforter up to my nose. *No, I didn't kill him,* I told the voice of reason in my head. *But I wanted to. Oh, how I wanted to.* And I knew I had to stay away from Macklin, because if I caught him again someplace in the dark, just the two of us, I didn't want to think about what might happen.

CHAPTER SEVEN
Thursday

Thursday morning found me churning up and down the fast lane of the pool at the Oak Bay Rec, trying to burn off those extra pounds. I enjoy swimming — once you find the rhythm, your arms and legs seem to remember what to do by themselves. Then you can release your mind and, as popular wisdom has it, go with the flow. I released mine to think about Perry. And the delinquent Tess.

I decided I was fed up with both the Misses

Eldon. Despite my admonition, Perry had told me a lie and I was still ticked about that. Did she think I wouldn't find out about the trust fund? Why on earth would she want to conceal that information from me? It was extremely important — it made a lot of pieces fall into place.

As for Tess, I didn't believe for a moment that some persuasive piece of feminist dogma had sent her fleeing to the arms of her new-found sisters. Ideas can be powerful, but not that powerful. None of the runaways I had ever dealt with had taken to their heels because of something they had learned in school. No, I believed the motive for her flight was something else. And if I did enough digging, I was sure I'd find it. Of course, I wasn't being paid to find it, just to bring Tess home. Or, at the very least, get her away from her friends during this full moon. At which time, presumably, they would all grow fangs and claws and turn into werewolves.

I had a lot of questions for Perry — questions she would soon get a chance to answer. After my late-night adventure with Macklin and Pansy, I had put a message on Perry's answering machine telling her to meet me at eight this morning.

When I had swum half a mile, I hauled myself out, dried and dressed, and headed for my stakeout of Concordia Books at the bakery across the street. I figured I deserved an apple fritter while I waited — after all, I *had* swum half a mile. As Francis had remarked, everything costs.

Perry showed up at eight on the dot in her slate gray deliveryperson's uniform, a brown envelope in her hand, a worried look on her face.

"Sit," I said, indicating the chair across the table.

She put the envelope down and sat, arms crossed protectively across her chest.

"Why didn't you tell me about Tess's trust fund?" I demanded.

She sighed audibly. "Because I was sure you'd think my only reason for wanting her back was to get my hands on her money."

"So what if I did? It wouldn't affect how hard I'd work. Why you want her back is your business. But don't lie to me, Perry. You tie my hands when you do. I need facts. Don't decide for me which ones are relevant and which aren't. One more lie and I drop this case."

"Yeah. Sorry," she muttered.

"And don't 'sorry' me," I fumed. "As a matter of interest, *did* you want to get your hands on her money?"

Perry looked stricken. "Of course not. At least, not in the way you put it. Tess knew that once she turned eighteen and was eligible for the first installment of her trust, we were going to see the trustees to work out a formal financial arrangement. This wasn't news to her."

"What kind of 'formal financial arrangement?' "

"You know — how the trust would pay Tess's school expenses, her rent, her car payments and insurance. That kind of thing. Tess knew all this," she reiterated. "That can't have been why she ran away. Her trust fund just doesn't have anything to do with all this. That's why I didn't tell you."

"Oh? Don't you think that fifty thousand dollars would be mighty attractive to Tess's new friends, the ones you think are so crazy?"

Perry looked ill.

I continued. "And here's a happy thought: I'm assuming Tess *could* take the money in a lump if she wanted to."

She opened and closed her mouth several times. "Yeah," she said weakly, at last. "But we agreed —"

"Screw your agreement. Tess evidently decided to do something different."

Perry glowered at me. "You make her sound like a criminal."

"Hey, Perry," I said. "Relax. I'm on your side. And I think it's more important than ever that Tess be separated from her new friends. What they plan to do at the full moon is only one of our worries."

"You're right," Perry said. "Sorry."

"Okay. I want you to phone Tess's trustees and find out what arrangement she's made to receive the money. See if you can get them to stall. They probably won't. If they won't, then call your attorney and find out how you can tie up the money: file a suit against Tess for back rent. Or tuition. Something. Anything. But it has to be done today."

She shook her head. "I don't have an attorney. Dad's attorney — the one who sort of looked after everything when my parents died — retired last year."

I scribbled a number on a paper napkin. "Call this lady — Virginia Silver. She's an old friend of mine. Tell her I told you to phone. She'll help."

Perry stuffed the napkin in her pocket. "I think I better call in sick until we get this straightened out." She stood up and stuck out her hand. "Thanks. I'm going home to make phone calls. Where can I get in touch with you?"

"I don't know. I'll be in and out. Just stay put and I'll call you."

I grabbed the brown envelope Perry had given me and hustled myself across the street to the bookstore. Tess was beginning to sound as though she didn't have both oars in the water. I mean, who would give fifty thousand dollars to a bunch of people you'd met in *class*, for God's sake? Of course I was speculating here, but it was beginning to seem more and more likely.

Another happy thought had occurred to me as I was talking to Perry, but this one I decided to keep to myself. I wondered just how free Tess was to leave her lair at Land's End, even if she wanted to.

Fifty thousand dollars. Forget the spiritual journey. Perry had said that the ladies of Land's End were planning some *event,* something that would act as an incentive to get the police moving on the Full Moon Rapist case. So how would fifty thousand dollars help? Did they plan to buy a Stinger missile and blow up Metro police headquarters? Maybe. Hell, nothing would surprise me. But there was no doubt that Tess would be well out of it. Whatever it was.

Marge was ministering to her window full of African violets when I walked through the door of the bookstore. George Winston's "Winter into Spring" was playing softly in the background, and I felt my blood pressure drop by about twenty points. Marge and Concordia always have that effect on me. A tall, stately woman with to-hell-with-it gray hair, Marge was fond of soft greens, turquoises, fuchsias. Today she was dressed in a long wool skirt of teal and aqua, an off-white wool turtleneck, aqua socks and Birkenstocks, a string of fat turquoise beads around her neck. She saw me come in and waved.

"Coffee's on," she said. "Help yourself. Bring me a cup, too, while you're at it."

I ambled toward the back of the bookstore, past the shelves of mysteries, science fiction, and biographies, through the children's books, and into the storeroom-cum-office in the back. A fat ginger cat looked up from his breakfast of kibble and eyed me curiously, wondering if he knew me.

"Morning, Rufus," I said. "How's business? Eaten any good books lately?"

Offended by my reference to his short-lived kittenish penchant for teething on the new arrivals, he turned his back and continued to crunch. As I recalled, he had demolished *Cosmos*, *The Handmaid's Tale*, and *A Pictorial Tour of Victoria's Gardens* before his adult teeth came in. Acknowledging my affront to his feelings, I bent down to pet him. "Sorry, guy. How are you getting along with the bibliophiles of Victoria? Lots of stimulating literary conversations?" Mollified, Rufus arched against my hand and butted my ankles, purring rustily. I scratched his ears and straightened up to pour coffee.

Marge finished her plant preening and I took a stool in front of the shelf marked RUFUS RECOMMENDS. Marge uses Rufus as a legitimate business expense — his photo adorns all her newspaper ads which feature him deep in contemplation of the latest best seller. Marge even lists him on her tax form as Concordia's advertising and public relations consultant. So far, Revenue Canada hasn't disagreed.

"If you stick around, I have a new edition of Hopkins you might like to see," she told me. Marge knows my weaknesses and keeps me tempted, and my checking account drained, with a steady stream of books.

I shook my head. "Thanks, but I can't. I'll come look at it later. Right now I need you to tell me about Diana McNeil."

"Oh." She took a seat on the steps leading up to the non-fiction section and propped her chin in her hands. "Okay. Let's see. Fascinating. Smart. Articulate. Accomplished. But a little odd."

"Marge, everyone's odd. What's different about Diana McNeil?"

"She disturbed me," Marge said. "She's unsettling. That's the best word I can think of. Once you get past the polite exterior, the surface — that is, if she lets you — you become aware of the most amazing thing. She seems to have a flame burning someplace inside her and when she talks to you, really *talks* to you, it's as though she's leading you by the hand toward the fire. She has these spooky pale eyes — wolf's eyes — and once she turns them on you, you can't look away. It's extraordinary."

"Wow. Quite a description." Privately, I wondered if maybe all this intensity wasn't chemically induced — an antidote to grief. Stranger things had happened.

Marge continued, "She's a most unusual woman,

Caitlin. I can see why her students adore her. Attention from her must be devastatingly flattering to an eighteen-year-old."

"Unsettling." I repeated Marge's word. "I take it she unsettled you?"

"As a matter of fact she did," she admitted. "The evening of her reading, she got here a little early and someone formally introduced us. I began to ask her some questions. You know, routine things — after all, I had to introduce her. But I must have said something that interested her because she suddenly became very focused on me. Very intent on what I was saying. Her eyes seemed to . . . hold me. Like I told you, Caitlin, I couldn't look away. We continued to talk, but I had the oddest feeling that she was not really listening to me. That she was . . . searching." Marge shivered and rubbed her arms. "It's as though she *wanted* something from me, looked for it, then simply dismissed me when she didn't find it."

"What do you mean, 'dismissed you?' ?"

Marge shrugged. "She smiled politely, ended the conversation and walked away."

"Whew."

"Yes."

"Do you remember what you were talking about?"

Marge shook her head. "Not really. Her new book, I suppose."

"Do you have a copy?"

"Sure. Right here." She got up, reached over my shoulder, and handed me a fat volume entitled *Warrior Women.* I opened it to the Table of Contents. The first section was a discussion of women warriors throughout history and I was surprised to see alongside the familiar names a host of unfamiliar ones: the Irish Medb, Camilla the Amazon, the Assyrian Semiramis, Tomuyris of the Massagetae, and many other women I had never heard of.

The second part of the book seemed to be a theoretical discussion of archetypes modern women live by, and the third, a discussion of how we can return to our former glory as warriors.

"Interesting stuff," I remarked. "Does she teach this?"

Marge nodded. "Apparently. Each of her courses has something to do with women warriors or heroines or female archetypes."

"Hmmmm," I said, an idea forming in my mind. "Sell me this, okay?" I handed over a twenty and Marge made change.

"Anything else you can tell me about her? Any close friends? Who introduced her to you?"

"One of her students. As for close friends, I don't know. She came by herself and left alone."

"Where does she live?"

"Out of town someplace — she said it took her forty-five minutes to drive here. I don't know exactly where. Sorry."

"No problem," I told Marge. "I guess I'll just go talk to her directly."

Marge cocked her head and smiled. "Watch it, Caitlin," she teased. "She admires strong women."

I snorted. "No danger here," I said ruefully. "I'm a hundred-and-forty pound weakling." Well, maybe a hundred and forty-one or so these days, I amended mentally.

Marge walked me to the door. "Don't be silly.

You have the kind of strength she admires in the women she writes about."

I was embarrassed and as I so often do at such times, I took refuge in adolescent humor. "Sure," I said. "I'll sweep her off her feet. She'll fall into my arms. Then she can feel my biceps and swoon."

The air should have prickled with ozone, and lightning should have struck, signifying prophesy. I couldn't have come closer to the truth if I'd tried.

At the provincial office of Lands and Titles, my old buddy Alistair McLaughlin was at his usual desk, pipe between his teeth, ashes on his vest, blueprints in a stack on a table beside him. Alistair is Records Chief for the northern part of the Saanich Peninsula. I hailed him from across the counter and he waved me back into the inner sanctum.

"I saw Niall yesterday," he informed me, referring to my former boss at the Crown Prosecutor's office. "He's looking a bit frayed around the edges. You're well out of that place, Caitlin."

"Sometimes I wonder," I replied. "At least with the CP I had frustration *and* a pension plan."

"Ah well, retirement isn't everything. The way Niall's going, he'll be too burned up to enjoy it. He's even given up golf," Alistair said in amazement. "Can you imagine that?"

I couldn't, although I personally feel that golf is one of the world's dumbest pastimes. When you realize that golf is "flog" spelled backwards, you begin to suspect that the Scots might have more of a sense of humor than they're credited with. After all, they invented hurling, haggis, and bagpipes, didn't they?

"So what can I do for you today?" Alistair asked.

"Land's End. I need to see a plat map. Then I might need some landowners' names."

"Land's End," he said thoughtfully, getting up to fetch a fat bunch of rolled blueprints. He spread them out on his table, weighting the edges with books. "Now that's an odd place. There's really no town there any more. It used to be a great summer retreat for the well-to-do. Since the war, it's become just a bunch of old run-down estates. Most of them are in receivership. See all this forest? It's Crown land. These places — here, here, and here — are youth camps. They lease the land. Use the places mostly in the summer." He sucked on his pipe. "Do you know there was a Saudi gentleman in town last winter who wanted to buy it? Estates, camps, Crown land — everything?" He snorted. "We made it so difficult for him that he went home. So," he said, "what do you want to know?"

I looked at the map in dismay. "I don't know. There's supposed to be a commune or something up there, and I was hoping a look a the map would show me something big enough to qualify. But all these places are big. I hardly know where to start."

"Well, now, let's see," he said. "I'd rule out the camps. Ditto for the forest land. That leaves the old run-down estates, and there are only a dozen or so. Unless the commune is operating illegally — you know, squatting on one of the old estates — there ought to be a transfer of title. Let's see what we have in the records."

We went back to his desk and booted up his computer. After a few moments of clicking and clacking, he informed me with satisfaction, "Bingo. There were three title transfers about a year back. And that's significant, because there's been nothing at all for, oh, decades. Even though they're falling to rack and ruin, those bloody places run at about a million apiece. No one can afford them."

"Except the Saudis," I commented.

"Too bloody true." He hit a button and a printer clattered to life. "Here you go," he said, ripping the paper out of the printer and handing it to me. "The new owners."

I looked over the names but they meant nothing to me. "The other estates — the ones that haven't changed hands recently — isn't *anyone* living on them? Caretakers and so on?"

He scratched an earlobe. "Some, I suppose. I was up there once. On a fishing weekend. One of the other department heads — that lazy dog Crowley, over across the hall — owns one of them. It's a bloody white elephant, he says. Can't afford to keep it and can't afford to sell it. You might talk to him. He's a twit, but there's no reason for him not to tell you what you want to know."

"Okay, I will." I folded the list and put it in my pocket. "Thanks, Alistair."

* * * * *

"Land's End," Crowley the Twit mused, lacing his hands behind his head and staring out the window. A paunchy, fair-haired man of about forty, he was already balding. "I rue the day my dad willed me that property. I haven't been up there in over three years."

"What about upkeep?" I asked him. "It must be a pretty valuable asset." I smiled wryly. "At least the Saudis thought so."

He made a face. "Sod the Saudis. We just decided we didn't want to sell to them. McLaughlin had the devil's own time tracing the property owners," he said, eyes twinkling. "I think they got the message. As for upkeep, I hire a family from the village to go check on it every so often. They do repairs, keep trespassers away — that sort of thing. The other landowners have similar arrangements, I imagine. What's your interest?" He gave me a teasing, sidelong look, accompanied by an irritating male look-you-up-and-down once over. "Say, you're not fronting for the Saudis, are you?"

So this was why Alistair thought Crowley a twit — he fancied himself a ladies' man. Well, he was certainly barking up the wrong tree. "No. I'm trying to trace a group of people who may be living on one of the estates. It would be helpful if I talked to your caretaker. Could I have his name?"

Crowley shrugged. "I don't see why not." He wrote a name and phone number on a piece of paper and handed it to me. "Oh, don't waste your time with the husband — he's a useless old fart. Talk to the daughter. Callista. She's the one who really takes care of things." He eyed me again, wanting to waste time, to play those old boring dominance and desirability games. "Are you sure you're not fronting for the Saudis? We could talk about it over lunch."

"Trust me," I told him, getting up to go. "And thanks."

When we shook hands, he held mine for moments longer than necessary in order to give emphasis to his parting utterance. "Any time," he said, infusing those two words with meaning no female over the age of nine could have missed. "Any time."

I disengaged from Crowley feeling a familiar irritation which stayed with me all the way to the parking lot. There, a flurry of fat raindrops changed my irritation to downright annoyance and I drove out onto Fort Street muttering under my breath.

Men.

It was mid-morning at U Vic and students were just changing classes. Still feeling irked, I walked into Emily Carr Hall where a quick job of detection informed me that Diana McNeil had her office.

I stood aside to let a dozen or so students of both sexes go by, wondering as I always do when I come to the campus what the world is coming to. Neat, sensibly-dressed, articulate Julia Springer was surely an anomaly, for the kids who went frolicking by me were a sorry bunch indeed.

"Hey, like . . ."

"And then, after she goes 'No way, man!' he goes . . ."

"I mean, like, fuck, y'*know* . . .

Give me strength. The more I listen to young people, the more I fear for our language. Contrary to what many apologists for the young would have us believe, the youth of today are not enriching our language with their quaint patois, their witty neologisms coined to hide the mysteries of youth from us old fogies. Oh no. We can't understand them because they're almost inarticulate. Our language does not flow trippingly from their tongues. All these "likes" and "y'knows" and "I means" are verbal sleight-of-hand to hide a dreadful inability to translate thoughts into speech.

If I had been less preoccupied with my cultural musings, I would have paid more attention to where I was going. Instead, I hauled open the heavy wooden door of Emily Carr Hall and ran straight into the arms of a woman laden down with papers. Technically speaking, *she* ran into me, as I was the one standing holding the door and she was the one moving forward. If this had been a basketball game, the ref would have called a foul on her for sure.

"Oof," I said, as she ran into my open arms, her elbows hitting me in my midsection. Her papers flew every which way and for a minute we teetered, arms locked in an awkward embrace. Hurrying to disentangle, I took a half-step backward when, annoyingly and painfully, the heavy plank door swung closed on my heels, throwing *me* into *her* arms this time. I stumbled over a stack of her papers, hit my chin on her forehead, and bit my lip.

"Well, shit!" I exclaimed in pain.

She burst out laughing and, putting her hands on my shoulders, stepped back away from me. "Sorry," she said. "Hey, are you hurt?"

"Bit myself," I said, wincing. "Nothing actionable."

She raised an eyebrow. "It may not be actionable, but you have a lot of blood running down your chin. C'mon. There's a ladies' room for faculty just down the hall."

I let her lead me to the bathroom, but once there I demurred. "Thanks. I don't mean to sound ungrateful, but I can probably manage now." What I really wanted was privacy to look at my lip and see how much damage I had done. To my annoyance, she propelled me into the ladies' room ahead of her.

"Nonsense," she said. "I'll just make sure you're all right."

I shrugged. Hey, have it your way. At the nearest basin I rinsed my mouth and spat. Yes indeedy, there *was* a lot of blood. I rinsed and spat a few more times and pulled out my lip for inspection. Uh huh. Tooth marks. I mopped the mess off my chin, noting with irritation that blood had dribbled onto my turtleneck and my camel's hair blazer. Thoroughly irritated, I took off my jacket and was about to dab at the blood with a wet paper towel when my assailant put a hand on my arm.

"That won't help," she said, taking the blazer from me and looking at it critically. "You'll just make it worse."

I eyed her with dwindling patience. "Any suggestions?"

"Let me send it to the cleaners. After all, the accident was my fault. I should have been looking where I was going." She gave me a strange smile. A vulpine smile. Indeed, she had a fox's face, narrow and clever-looking, an aggressively curly mop of light brown hair underlaid with tints of flame and cinnamon, and pale, pale eyes. "And besides, one ought never to argue with a woman carrying a gun," she said.

My hand flew to my .357, holstered at the back of my pants. In all the excitement, I'd forgotten about it.

"So, what are you? A cop?" she asked.

I turned to look at her. We were standing so close I could see a flurry of dark flecks around the irises of her strange citrine eyes. "No," I answered. "I'm a private investigator."

"Ah," she breathed. "Of course."

Disconcerted, I blinked and looked away. The blazer lay on the counter between us, and as I reached for it, she put a hand on my arm.

"I mean it," she said. "Let me pay for having it cleaned. I can understand that you might want to wear it for a while longer though." She chuckled. "At least until you get off campus. Send me the bill, all right?"

I shrugged. "All right. Give me a name and address."

To my relief, she took her hand from my arm. "You can send it here, to the university. Women's studies department. My name is Diana McNeil."

From a chair against one wall of her minuscule office, I ran an exploratory tongue over my wounded lip and studied Diana McNeil.

"Tess Eldon," she said, leaning back in her swivel

chair. The light through the window behind her kept her face in shadow. I didn't like that, so I got up and moved my chair to a better vantage point. I like to see people's faces. Diana raised an eyebrow but made no comment. "Well, she's registered in both my classes. She got an A on the first exam and an A on her oral presentation. She seems bright, interested, articulate." She frowned. "I might be more helpful if you told me what you wanted to know."

I ignored that for the time being. "Is she still attending classes?"

"I don't take attendance, but let me think. Yes, I believe she was in class last time."

"I'd like your permission to come to class tomorrow or whenever your class meets next. I need to talk to Tess and this seems the best bet."

Diana made an expansive gesture. "By all means do come. Can you tell me what this is all about? Is Tess in some kind of trouble?"

"I'm working for Tess's sister," I said, trying to tell her as little as possible. I had more questions I needed to ask, and I didn't want to spook her. "It's a . . . family matter."

"Oh."

"Have you noticed any changes in Tess since she enrolled in your classes?"

"Changes? I'm not sure what you mean."

"Appearance, behavior — that kind of thing."

She smiled. "Miss Reece, college students are in a continual state of change. They pick up and discard ideas as quickly as they change socks. And they ought to be encouraged to do this. College is the place of intellectual exploration."

I felt patronized. Lectured to. Evidently she

figured the closest I had come to college was the faculty ladies' room. Must be my thuggish vibes — if so, Diana wasn't the first to have noticed them. Miffed, I continued. "What can you tell me about Tess? Her friend says that she found your course to be particularly stimulating. So much so that she changed her program, dropped her best friend, and ran away from home. That's one heck of a lot of intellectual exploration."

Diana placed her elbows on the desk, made a little tent of her fingers, and looked over them at me. Stalling, I thought. Interesting. "Surely you don't think my *class* had something to do with her running away?"

I shrugged. "I agree that it seems unlikely. But it's the best lead I have. Nothing else seems to have happened to her around that time — no religious experience, no fight with her family, no breakup with her boyfriend. Nothing like that."

"Just my class."

"Just your class. And some people she met there." I waited, but Diana didn't rise to the bait. Well, what had I expected? After all, she was the kids' professor, not their troop leader. Maybe she didn't know a thing about the study group. Or the commune.

A knock sounded on Diana's office door just then, and a tall redhead in a blue pullover and faded jeans burst into the room, flung open the door, hiding me where I sat in the corner. "Diana, I have some great news!" she said gleefully.

Diana held up a hand, interrupting her. "Not now. I have a visitor, Gillian," she said quietly.

The redhead turned and noticed me. "Oops," she

said, blushing. "Sorry. I'll come back later." She backed out the door.

"Please do," Diana said coolly. "Sorry about that," she told me as the door closed. "That was Gillian. My research assistant. She tends to be a little, well, exuberant."

"Mmmm," I said, my mind racing. I had seen that tall redhead somewhere before. But where?

"So you'd like to come to class in the hopes of talking to Tess?" Diana asked, bringing me back to the present. "Well, I don't think that will be any problem. Class meets tomorrow."

"Thanks," I told her. "What time?"

"Ten o'clock. Room two-oh-four, just down the hall."

I got up to go. "Okay. Thanks again."

Diana came around from behind the desk and perched on a corner. She looked up at me, an unreadable expression on her face. "Miss Reece, do private investigators believe in private justice?"

"I beg your pardon?"

"Forgive me, but I'm interested in what someone like you believes."

"Someone like me?" Ye gods, was this another Tonia? Someone like me, indeed.

"Yes. Someone who does the kind of work you do. What *are* you dedicated to? Mercy? Justice?"

I laughed. "Justice? Not any more."

"Oh? Does that mean you once were?"

I leaned against the wall and thought about her question. After a fleeting moment in which I considered saying something glib, I decided to tell her the truth. "I served justice once. As a prosecuting attorney in the CP's office. It was a very unsatisfactory relationship, so I ended it. As for mercy, well that's something I've not thought much about." I shrugged. "Why do you want to know what I believe in?"

"Because what you do intrigues me. If you serve neither mercy nor justice, what do you serve?"

I laughed uneasily. Where was this conversation going? "What makes you think I serve anything?"

"Because I sense that you do," she said simply. "We all serve something. Whose acolyte are you?"

"No one's."

"Why is that?" she asked.

I blinked. How had this conversation begun? I only wanted her permission to come to class, not a philosophical discussion about mercy and justice, for God's sake. Irked, I jammed my hands in my blazer pockets and snorted. "You know, you have the wrong idea about me," I told her. "Maybe I specialize in finding lost dogs or spying on philandering spouses. That's not very intriguing. And as for whose acolyte I am, well I serve my checking account. I'm a private investigator. A gumshoe. A snoop. Someone people pay to do their dirty work."

"That's not what you are at all," she said with certainty, standing up to face me. We weren't the same height, and as she raised her head to look at me I saw with a *frisson* of fear what Marge Sherman had been talking about. There was a predatory avidity about Diana that made my scalp prickle. I felt like the fly in the spider's parlor. If this had been a century earlier, I would have been making signs to ward off the evil eye.

"Oh yes I am," I insisted, some imp of perversity making my lip curl in a sneer. "I'm just paid muscle. Curiosity for hire. A thug."

To my immense surprise, she threw back her head and laughed. "A thug. How perfect." Then, when she looked at me again, she was only . . . Diana. Gone was the strange intensity I thought I had seen in her eyes earlier. I sighed with relief. For that matter, had it ever really been there? *Lighten up,* I scolded myself. *You need lunch. Nothing like a cholesterol and sugar fix to dispel the vapors.*

"Ten o'clock tomorrow," I said. As I reached for the door I noticed, tacked to the back of the door, some lines of a poem in Latin — with a little Greek thrown in near the end — neatly transcribed in a calligraphic hand. I felt suddenly irritated by all this bullshit. Acolytes and Latin poems — give me a break! Knowing that I was peeved because I felt outclassed, I growled my way out of her office. "Thanks," I called ungraciously over my shoulder.

"You're welcome, I'm sure," she called after me in a voice filled with amusement.

I muttered to myself all the way out to the parking lot.

"Latin and Greek, for God's sake," I complained to Repo as I changed clothes. "Who reads dead languages anymore?"

"Nraff," he commiserated from his tea-cozy position on the end of my bed.

I tossed the camel's hair blazer over a chair,

108

peeled off my turtleneck and exchanged it for a T-shirt and a lavender wool pullover. "The worst thing about it was I know darned well I read that poem once, back in the good old days when I had my wits about me," I told him. I sat on the end of the bed beside him, stroking his pelt. "But can I remember it? No way. Am I getting past it, Fur Face? My brain must have more holes in it than Swiss cheese. Why, I used to be able to —"

The sounds of Repo's snores answered me. Life was pretty grim when even your cat was bored with your breast-beating.

I patted the sleeping feline ingrate, plucked my windbreaker from the hall tree, and trudged out to my moribund MG. A fit companion, I thought, as I coaxed it into reluctant life. Neither of us is firing on all cylinders. *Ave atque ale!* I called over my MG's noise, childishly pleased that I had dredged up something from my long-gone classical education. But why this — the gladiators' greeting to Caesar, their way of thumbing their noses at death. *Ave atque ale: those about to die salute you.* I shrugged. I wasn't responsible for my memory. To the accompaniment of a salute of automotive farts, I hit the road for Land's End.

As I wheeled out of the Golden Arches, sipping the last of my chocolate shake, I unfolded my map of the Saanich Peninsula and consulted it at stoplights between slurps. Land's End lay due north of the city, past the airport, through Saanich and Sidney, past the small Anacortes ferry terminal that linked Vancouver Island to the U.S., and the huge Swartz Bay terminal that connected us to the British Columbia mainland. Just as its name stated, it was Land's End — a stubby, three-mile-long finger-shaped spit jutting into the ocean immediately north of Deep Cove, the most northerly point on the Saanich peninsula.

I cruised through Saanich and Sidney, and just before I got to the busy Swartz Bay ferry terminal, I turned west, away from the water, onto Land's End Road. The road led on past a gas station, a convenience store, and a cluster of houses, then up a little hill and into a fir forest. As I descended the other side of the hill, I saw with dismay that civilization stopped here. Twenty yards ahead, the asphalt petered out and a rutted dirt track began. I shifted down into first, but after a half-mile of bouncing along the dirt road, skirting holes big enough to swallow my car entirely, I decided to spare my old MG, and my rear end. As I sat there at a bend in the so-called road, idling my engine in the green gloom, muttering to myself, I heard the telltale sounds of something big shifting gears and approaching entirely too fast.

"Shit," I said, looking around. There was barely room for two cars to pass, if they crawled past one another. But whatever was hurtling toward me was definitely not crawling. So I took the course of least resistance and drove off the road into a squishy mess of moss, ferns, and mud. And just in time, too. A black Blazer came hurtling around the bend, occupying every inch of the space where my MG had sat scant moments before. As it tore by me, I saw the wide, startled blue eyes of the female driver.

"You asshole!" I yelled in its wake. The Blazer sped on. But not before I got part of the license number — MCE 9-something — and recognized the blue and white U Vic parking sticker plastered on its bumper.

It took me a good half hour of backing, filling, and pushing to free my MG from the grip of the forest primeval. When I was finished, I had moss and mud up to my knees, and the beginnings of a truly monumental headache. Turning my car around, I drove back to the little store at the side of the road and, with guilty thoughts of my diet, bought two Mars bars and a Diet Pepsi. As I took my purchases to the cashier — a downtrodden-looking, overweight young woman with bad skin, scraggly hair, too-tight jeans, and a grey sweatshirt that said BORN TO SHOP — I decided to do a little fishing.

"This must be a nice quiet place to work," I said as I handed over two bucks.

"Quiet?" She looked at me as though I had made an indecent suggestion. "Dead is more like it. We don't have any traffic through here — it all goes to Swartz Bay. Land's End Road goes, like noooowhere." She put down the magazine she had been reading and started to ring up my purchases. "Believe me, I wouldn't be working here if my dad didn't own the place. He insists that I contribute" — eye-rolling here — "to the family business."

"Mmmm," I commiserated, unwrapping a candy bar. "If it's so quiet, where'd that black Blazer come from then? It almost ran me off the road."

She gave me my change and her face took on an unpleasant smirk. Plainly she was bursting with information. "For one thing, it's a Bronco, not a

Blazer and for another, she always drives like that."
She actually sniffed with disapproval. "Usually it's
packed with at least four or five women. They never
stop in here to buy gas or anything — think they're
too good for us, I guess. But I know what they're up
to."

"Oh yeah?" I asked, trying not to show my
interest.

"Yeah. I got to wondering, so I asked around a
little. They must've rented one of the big estates out
on the point because they're sure staying there. The
four or five broads in the Bronco live there now,
God knows why, and the other ones come up on
weekends."

"The other ones?"

She nodded sagely. "Two or three others. They
come up about suppertime on Fridays, just like
clockwork. In a red Geo Storm."

"Wow," I said in admiration. "What do you
suppose they do?"

She looked both ways, leaned across the counter
and whispered, "I figured it out. Drugs. And weird
sex. They're dykes, right? Isn't that what dykes do?"

I inhaled my Pepsi. "Is it?" I croaked, in between
bouts of coughing.

"Sure," she said, conspiratorially. "I saw two of
them in the Bronco one night when they had to slow
down out front and wait for a truck. They were
kissing! Gross. That's how I know they're dykes."

"No!" I exclaimed in mock horror. "Kissing? My
God, what is the world coming to?"

Born to Shop laughed an ugly laugh, the prurient

little homophobe. Plainly my sarcasm was lost on her. "Yeah well, lucky for them they have Callie Jubal for a friend — she's got to be letting them stay there on the sly. Although, come to think of it, she's probably a dyke, too." She eyed me speculatively. "What do you suppose they *do?*" she asked, eyes bright. I suddenly amended my opinion of her. Here was a closet case if ever I saw one.

"Who? The Jubals?"

"No, the dykes! You know, in bed. I've always wondered."

"Beats me," I told her, tossing my Pepsi can and candy bar wrapper in the trash. "Probably what the rest of the world does. Although I've heard dykes have more fun."

She looked so crestfallen, I almost recommended a couple of books, but then I remembered the ugly laugh that had preceded her revelation about Callie Jubal.

"Gotta go," I said. "Nice talking to you."

"Yeah," she sighed, and returned to her perusal of *Soap Opera Digest*.

At a depressingly yuppie-looking cafe just past the ferry terminal, I ordered the chowder and, with a certain amount of trepidation, the hot fish salad. The restaurant was almost empty — it was just before four — so the hostess probably figured my muddy pants and shoes wouldn't scare away customers. She seated me in a corner behind a

thicket of potted trees, but I foiled her plans. No
sooner had she hidden me in the foliage than I
bounded out of the underbrush to use the phone.

"Oak Bay Camera Shop," answered the familiar
voice.

"Hey Lester," I said. "How's life?"

"Caitlin! Life is great. What are you up to these
days?"

"Oh, the usual. Say, you probably own that place
by now, so getting away to do a little job for me
ought to be easy. Right?"

"Caitlin, for heaven's sake," he said, clearly
embarrassed. "Of course I don't own this place —
Mr. Henderson does. And you may recall, I haven't
graduated yet."

"I know. But I've heard from a friend at the
nursing home that Henderson may not recover from
this last stroke. He has no family and he was
always crazy about you. So who do you think he
plans to leave the store to in his will, hmmm?"

"Me," Lester said. "I know. He told me last year."

"So what's there to be sad about?"

"Well, the thing is, I don't know if that's what I
want. I mean the store does a good business and
everything, but it's not very exciting. I don't think
I'm cut out to be a shopkeeper. After all, my major
is journalism."

"Phooey to that," I said. "Chasing stories really
isn't all that exciting. It's mostly a lot of dull
background research, and interviews with inarticulate
salt-of-the-earth types. Then, if you're lucky, they'll

send you off to cover the occasional house fire in Sooke. Big deal."

"Sounds fine to me," he said cheerfully. "I just want to see my byline."

"Spoken like a true reporter," I sighed. "You're all hopeless egomaniacs. Your byline, indeed."

"Thank you for that piece of advice, Ann Landers," he said. "Now, what did you want from me?"

"Oh, nothing much. I need to borrow your Jeep and your photographic abilities for a little while tomorrow."

"Oh yeah? Where are we going?"

"Land's End. I've just come from there and the road's a killer. How are your shocks?"

"Well, let me think," he said fussily. "I'm sure they're okay. The Jeep just had a fifteen-thousand-mile checkup. So what kind of photos will you need?"

"Black and white prints."

"Okay. I'll get the film. What time?"

"I have to be at U Vic at ten, so why don't we meet about eleven thirty at British Fish 'n Chips?"

"Sounds good," he said. "One thing, though. Um, last time I did you a favor I got run off the road. My Suzuki was totaled. I like this new Jeep a lot and —"

"Listen, we're just going to take a drive," I soothed him. "We'll look at some property, shoot some photos. Nothing could be safer. Of course, if it's your safety you're worried about . . ." I teased him.

"Hey!" he bristled predictably. "Who said I was worried about my safety? I was thinking of my car. My friend Rob has a banged-up Land Rover but it has four-wheel drive and great suspension. I'd rather bring that. If you don't mind."

"I don't care. Just as long as my hindquarters don't feel every rock from Land's End to the point."

"No. It — er, they — won't. And just for my information, who will we be impersonating tomorrow? I need to get in the spirit of things."

"Realtors," I told him. "We'll be looking at some property for a prospective client. A big client. Those estates out on Land's End run well over a million each."

"Sounds like fun," he said with boyish enthusiasm. "See you at eleven-thirty."

The chowder was still warm when I got back to my table, but that was about the only good thing I could say for it. To my horror, it was a bright coral color — exactly the hue you get when you mix cream of tomato soup with whole milk. Yech. Even as a child I declared I would rather eat dirt than pink soup. I tasted it, shuddered, and pushed the bowl guiltily to one side, nibbling a roll until the arrival of the hot fish salad. When my waitress delivered it, I found to my surprise that it was quite edible, nothing more ominous than a piece of grilled haddock atop a plateful of crisp green salad. I polished it off in no time, resisted dessert, paid the bill, and left.

In the parking lot I yawned and peered at my watch. Almost five. I needed to go on home, have a bath, and think. About Diana McNeil's research assistant Gillian, whom I had definitely seen before, about the wild women of Land's End, about Callie Jubal who was, apparently, clandestinely renting Crowley's estate to the aforementioned wild women, and about the Bronco that had nearly run me over. Well, perhaps I should make an early evening of it, I thought. A hot bath, a glass of Scotch, a little Purcell, a brace of warm cats. I was beginning to feel good when I suddenly recalled with a weary sigh that a little later, under the waxing moon, I had a date with the peripatetic Pansy. I slammed the car door and groaned. No way was I going to drive all the way home and get nice and comfy, only to drive all the way back to Saanich to play chase with a cat. Nope. I was getting the tuna now. Time to show that feline who was boss.

I parked in Wendy's driveway and got out cautiously to reconnoiter. The tuna can I had left on the porch was licked clean — a good sign, I told myself. I carried Gray's trap to the porch, loaded it, placed a freshly opened can of tuna on the trigger plate, and retired to my car to wait. I munched my way through the contents of a bag of Ruffles I had purchased along with the tuna, and sipped my Big Gulp of Diet Pepsi, trying to stay awake. Finally I gave up. Scrunching down in the seat, I got as comfortable as I could, and lowered my eyelids, intending to meditate for only a moment or two.

I was sure I had rested my eyes for maybe only five minutes, but when I opened them next, evening was well advanced. I sat up straight and scrubbed my hands through my hair, willing myself awake.

My tongue felt thick and furry, my nose was stuffy, and my bladder was suggesting a quick trip to the hamburger joint down the street. The streetlights had come on while I was napping, and by their eerie greenish light I could plainly see the trap on the front porch. I looked again. There was a little white cat inside that trap.

"Hot damn!" I exclaimed, getting out of the car and hustling to the porch.

The cat began hissing like a fractured steam pipe as soon as my feet hit the first step. By the time I was on the porch proper, bending over the cage solicitously, Pansy had escalated her warning from hisses and moans to bloodcurdling yowls. Clearly, she wasn't about to go down without a fight.

"Settle down, for heaven's sake," I said, quite at a loss to know what to do. "I'm on your side."

"Rrrreeee!" she shrieked.

"Jesus, someone's going to call the SPCA. Give me a break, Pansy," I coaxed as I carried the trap back to my car.

"Fffff, fffff, fffff," she said, blowing herself up for another round of screaming.

I put the cage behind the driver's seat on the floor, jumped into my MG, and drove for home as fast as the speed limit allowed. Someplace on the highway, Pansy settled into a mournful *sotto voce* keening, and we pulled into my driveway with Pansy crying "Ooo, ooo, ooo," from a corner of the cage. I felt like an ax-murderer as I carried the cage up the stairs and into the house.

Repo met me just inside the front door and as I put the cage down to take off my windbreaker, he eyed Pansy with great interest. "Hein?" he inquired companionably, stretching his neck to touch noses with the visitor.

Pansy, however, was having none of it. Fluffed to twice her size, she told Repo to get out of her face. "MrrrrAIR!" she hollered, attacking the mesh of the cage.

"Forget it, Repo," I told him when he backed off, plainly affronted. "It's not your technique. A skinny ex-con with a hammer adjusted her attitude last night. She may never like anyone again."

"Frritt?" Jeoffrey called anxiously.

Torn between excitement and duty, Repo left the hysterical Pansy and hurried to Jeoffrey's side. He licked the little tabby's head and ears and Jeoffrey settled down beside the armchair. Then Repo came to sit by my feet, looking up at me expectantly. "Ungow?" he inquired.

"Beats me," I told him. "Gray Ng would undoubtedly know what to do. All I know is that Pansy can't stay in this trap forever. If nothing else, she probably has to visit the litterpan."

"Yerf," Repo opined, regarding Pansy from a safe distance.

"What the heck, let's go for it." I reached down and opened the trap.

Pansy, who had been watching me with wary intelligence, saw her opening and took it. A white and apricot blur, she streaked out of the trap, hurdled the coffee table, vaulted over the back of the couch, and nimbly scaled a seven-foot bookcase. From the lofty heights of my Shakespeare collection, she looked down at us, gave one last, hopeless, hair-curling cry, then hunkered down, a lump of misery.

"Unnh," Repo said in astonishment.

"I agree," I told him. "Let's forget her for a while and have supper."

The doorbell rang just as I had dished out the last of the Little Bits o' Beef.

"Yeah?" I called to whoever was at the door.

"Oak Bay Florist," a voice answered.

Oh, sure, I thought suspiciously. *Tell me another one.* I flipped on the porch light, twitched the curtain aside, and took a look. A young guy of about seventeen stood there, a box in his arms. A white van with the name of the flower shop was parked at the curb. Everything looked safe enough. I opened the door and he handed me the box.

"Somebody spent a fortune on these," he said as I signed for the flowers. "Two dozen long-stemmed roses. *Red* roses."

I closed and locked the door after him, then took the flowers to the kitchen. Roses? For *moi?* I wasn't aware I had any admirers. I opened the box and took a look at the card that accompanied it. It said:

Looking forward to knowing you better.
Dee.

I snorted in disgust. Just as I had suspected, the flowers had been sent to the wrong address. I knew no one named Dee. I ran for the front door, but the van had already pulled away.

"What the hell," I told Repo who was busy pulling the petals off a rose and eating them one by one in evident enjoyment. "Let's pretend someone named Dee wants to know us better."

"Yerf," he agreed, and began to wash.

Tossing the box in the trash, I put the roses in an empty one-gallon milk container. I looked around for a moment, trying to decide where to put them, then carried them to the coffee table, holding one of the blooms for a moment in my palm. The color of burgundy wine, the rose had a black velvet sheen that was unearthly. I closed my eyes and brought it to my face, touching it for an instant to my lips, savoring it, breathing deeply, allowing my lungs to be filled with its sweetness. Then I sighed and straightened up. Whoever she was, Dee certainly had good taste, I thought with a pang. Roses — the ultimate romantic gesture.

I stirred the bath water with my foot and sank into it with a grunt of delight. After supper, Repo had escorted Jeoffrey to the litterpan and to bed. Then he stationed himself at the bottom of the bookcase where Pansy was keeping her vigil.

"Is this a good idea?" I asked him. "What if she's threatened by your ferocious male presence?"

"Naff," he said confidently, closing his eyes and settling in for a vigil of his own.

"Among them be it," I muttered, and went to run my bath.

Now, wallowing in the warm water, I took another swallow of Scotch, leaned my head against the back of the tub and spread the hot, wet washcloth over my face.

What a day. I'd learned that Tess Eldon was an heiress, Perry Eldon was a liar, the wild women of Land's End were dykes, the Bronco driver was a maniac, Callie Jubal was a thief, and Diana McNeil was a fruitcake. God, why couldn't I just once meet nice, normal people? I thought about the exchange between Diana and Gillian and tried to call Gillian's face up again in my memory. Where had I seen her before? I yawned and let my mind roam, dozing a little. And then it came to me. I had seen both Gillian and the woman driving the Bronco, and recently too. Monday night in fact. Gillian had been the redhead in the black cape — the one who had stopped me as I crossed the campus — and the blonde woman was one of her cohorts.

"Ha!" I exclaimed, sitting upright. I had just remembered something else — a piece of paper Gillian had shoved into my hands. But what had I done with it?

I didn't find the piece of paper in the back of my MG as I had hoped, but I did find the brown envelope Perry had given me this morning. I definitely needed to take a look at that.

The other piece of paper would turn up. I made myself a plate of cheese, crackers, salmon pate, and pickles, poured a little more Scotch and carried my makeshift dinner on a tray into the living room. I popped Purcell's "Dido and Aeneas" into the tape player and munched, feeding a few bites of salmon to Repo now and then. That's when it hit me. The piece of paper was in the back pocket of the jeans I had been wearing Monday. Sure enough, buried in the nest of fusty clothes in my laundry basket were the jeans. And the piece of paper.

I carried the paper — it was a flyer, really — into the living room and unfolded it, smoothing it out on the couch beside me.

WOMEN: NEED AN ESCORT?

the flyer asked. It talked about the campus rapes and suggested that if women banded together, they could keep each other safe. It blathered on a bit more about sisterhood, then came to the point. Women could, if they wanted, call the Daughters of Artemis (whose phone number was printed on the bottom of the flyer) and arrange to be escorted to and from night classes. It was all terribly earnest and terribly nineteen-seventies. I tossed the flyer onto the coffee table.

So Gillian and the blonde Bronco driver were members of this escorting group, were they? And presumably there were other Daughters as well — the rest of the wild women of Land's End. Was this Tess's study group? I guessed so. The escorting and the rest of the fun and games the Daughters had planned were probably the mind-expanding activities that had led Tess to flee from her nice, middle-class home on Beach Drive. So what was it — the kid just craved excitement?

I sat back, stroking Repo and thinking about Tess. Maybe their paramilitary demeanor and their underlying militancy, their *Women Unite!* and *Disarm Rapists!* thinking had had a great influence on Tess. A militant sisterhood was, after all, a very seductive idea. Still . . . I frowned. As an explanation, something didn't jibe. It felt incomplete.

I emptied the brown envelope onto the coffee table, and a photo fell out. A five-by-seven glossy of a freckle-faced girl of about sixteen with kinky blonde hair and braces. A note affixed to the photo said: "Tess. Taken two years ago." Written on a sheet of paper was Julia Springer's name, and the titles of Diana's courses. That was it.

"Jesus," I said to Repo, "pretty slim pickings."

He pricked up his ears, said "Mmmph" out of politeness, then resumed eyeing the salmon. I had a few more bites, then gave him the can, which he cleaned in no time flat. He sighed, gave his coat a few perfunctory licks, then settled against me for a snooze. I put my head back and studied the ceiling.

A militant sisterhood. Yes indeed, that had a certain appeal. Amazons united against the foe, riding into battle with bows drawn and breasts bared. I snorted. Unfortunately the foes women had to fight today couldn't be felled so easily. But the appeal was there, nonetheless.

As Repo snored softly beside me, I drifted with Purcell's crisp music through Aeneas's arrival in Carthage, and the inevitable, doomed attraction between him and Queen Dido. Then, just as love (or something akin to it) blossomed, the gods began to punish the lovers. I listened as the Sorceress greeted her cronies, the witches:

"Wayward sisters, you that fright
The lonely traveler by night.
Who, like dreadful ravens crying,
Beat the windows of the dying,
Appear! Appear at my call, and share in the
    fame
Of a mischief shall make all Carthage flame.
Appear!"

Conjured by the Sorceress, the witches appeared, asking:

"Say, Beldame say, what's thy will?"

The Sorceress replies:

"Harm's our delight and mischief all our skill."

The resultant gleeful chorus in which witches and Sorceress joined their voices in a raucous, rollicking cackle had always made me smile. Until now. Tonight, for some reason, the laughter fell flat. I couldn't seem to get in the mood. So when the witches sang the echoing chorus of Act One, Purcell's moody, heavy melody lay on my spirit like a physical weight. More than this, though, the words seemed ominous, portentous.

"In our deep vaulted cell, the charm we'll prepare,
Too dreadful a practice for this open air."

With a click, my tape player shut off. I sat there for a moment, feeling as though I had missed some important clue, feeling for one instant that something was approaching, something powerful, something ineluctable. Something that made my palms sweat and my heart race. But what? I closed my eyes, waiting for the moment to pass. From experience, I knew this phenomenon well — it was a rudimentary prescience, a gift from the distaff side of my family, something I had inherited along with my hair color and blood type. And this sixth sense was telling me to beware. I appreciated the warning, but did it always have to try to frighten me to death? I guessed so. And I knew, too, that I had only to wait, and this atavistic dread would pass. It did. In another moment, I sensed the huge, dark presence that waited for me someplace, sometime in my future, turn away from me. *Not yet,* it said. *Not yet.* I drew a ragged breath and wiped my hands on my sweats. Then, in a silence so loud it fairly hummed, I got up to turn off my stereo.

"C'mon, Fur Face," I called softly to Repo. "Let's go join Jeoffrey in the bedroom." On my way to the kitchen with my tray of salmon tin, pickle bottle, cheese and crackers, I noticed that Pansy had descended from her perch at some point during Act One and had devoured the dinner I'd left her. She was back on the bookcase, however, chin on folded paws, sleeping with one eye open. I was about to say something soothing to her when suddenly I heard a sound that drove all soothing thoughts out of my head. I heard the squeal of my back door opening.

"Macklin," I whispered and, putting my tray on a corner of the dining room table, I sprinted for my bedroom closet. I had the comforting heft of my .357 in my hand in about ten seconds and was back in the hall outside the kitchen in another five. Heart thudding, I dropped to my knees. And then I did just what my firearms instructor Brendan had expressly told his students not to do. I didn't wait for the son of a bitch to come to me. I went after him.

It was too late to turn out the light — Macklin would have seen it and realized I'd heard him. On hands and knees, I scuttled to my right, around the perimeter of the kitchen, ending up just in front of the stove. To my left was the open door which led to a little pantry on my back porch. It was the door leading from the pantry to the back porch that I had heard — its hinges squeaked. I took a deep breath and tried to slow my heartbeat. If he was coming in, I'd hear the boards creak as he crossed the pantry floor.

They creaked.

I rose to a crouch, assumed the Weaver position, and waited for him. His shadow came first, then his head and shoulders cleared the doorway. He, too, was crouched, and as I saw the dark figure hesitate in the doorway, my brain seemed to sizzle. I didn't want just to shoot him and have done with it. Oh no. I wanted to *hurt* him. Before I could stop myself, I drew my right leg back and kicked him in the head. Hard. I heard his teeth click as my foot connected, and with a cry he fell backwards in a heap in the pantry. I was on him in an instant, one hand in his hair, my .357 at his temple. I was so enraged I couldn't see straight, and if I hadn't heard the voice then, I might have pistol-whipped him. Or shot him.

"Please," the voice said, a voice that wasn't Macklin's. "Please."

Stunned, I let go my grip on his hair and spun the figure around. Shaking, weeping, blood running down her face, Diana McNeil fell to her knees and looked up at me.

"Oh, God," I said, and walked to the kitchen sink and vomited.

* * * * *

"Are you sure you don't want a doctor?" I asked her. "I really wish you'd let me take you to one. I have a friend —"

"I'm sure," she replied, interrupting me, holding a bag of ice to her face. "You did a fine job of first aid. My nose isn't broken — it just bled a lot."

"You'll have a couple of great black eyes tomorrow," I said. "And one wonderful headache. Jesus, you're going to look like you tangled with King Kong." I took a gulp of Scotch and noted that the shaking in my hands was getting worse, not better, the more alcohol I consumed. How very interesting.

"It's not me I'm worried about, it's you," Diana said.

"Me?" I croaked. "Hey, no need to worry about me. Let's worry about you instead. Do you know I could have broken your neck when I drop-kicked you? Or driven your septum clean through the back of your skull? God knows I intended to. And if you hadn't spoken up right when you did I might have thumped on your head a little with my .357 there." I nodded at it where it reposed on the coffee table between us. "And heck, then I might have shot you." I swallowed another mouthful of Scotch, noting that my lips had begun to quiver and my teeth to clack together. In short, I was coming unglued.

"What happened was my fault," she said firmly, putting the ice pack down on the coffee table. "When you didn't answer the front door, I thought I'd try the back. It just . . . opened."

I had to see for myself. A quick check of the back door showed me why it had "just opened."

Someone had broken my pantry window, wriggled through, and worked on the lock from the inside. Now the door would open and close, and the deadbolt would turn, but the lock wouldn't engage. And no one would know unless they examined it closely. This little stunt had Macklin written all over it. My hair rose as I realized he must have done it sometime today — I checked my doors and windows every night before I went to bed. So he'd found me — I'm in the book, after all. I fished around for a hammer and nails, nailed a board over the broken window, and secured the back door with a chair jammed under the knob. That would have to do for now.

"You know, I *did* call out," Diana said. Guiltily, I thought of Purcell and "Dido and Aeneas." Yeah, she probably had. Then she added quietly, "I wanted to see if you'd gotten my roses."

"Your roses?" I asked blankly. Then I remembered: the roses. The roses that had come from Dee. D for Diana. The florist had made a name out of an initial. Shit. "No problem," I told her with a brittle laugh. "That's the way I always greet people who send me roses. Just one of my little quirks."

"Caitlin," she said, getting up and coming to sit beside me, "just slow down." She took my hands in hers, but I pulled them free. I needed one hand to pour and one hand to drink.

"I thought you were someone else," I managed to force out from between my chattering teeth. "A rapist named Sean Macklin. I've been waiting for him — he said he was going to cut my heart out.

For sending him to prison. I prosecuted him."
Panicked, horrified, I took another drink, praying for
oblivion. But I was still on an adrenaline high and
the booze was making me twitch and babble. "I
could have killed you," I whispered. "Jesus, Diana, I
could have *killed* you."

"It was my fault," she said reassuringly, patting
my shoulder awkwardly. "Please don't be so hard on
yourself."

I poured myself another drink, realizing that this
might not be the wisest thing in the world. But
short of putting my .357 to my own head, I couldn't
think of anything else to do. I needed to escape,
damn it. I needed to not be Caitlin for a while. I
needed to not think about the feel of my foot
connecting with Diana's nose. And most of all, I
needed not to remember the horrible dark rush of
joy with which I had embraced Macklin/Diana, my
gun to his/her temple. I needed everything to just
. . . stop. Diana patted my shoulder again and I
twitched her hand away. Why in hell was she being
so nice? In fact, why was she still here?

"You're pretty calm for someone who was kicked
in the head and almost killed," I accused her. "Why
are you so goddamned calm? And why did you send
the goddamned roses, anyhow?"

"Don't assume I'm calm," she said, fixing me with
her eerie amber eyes. "Don't assume that at all. But
someone has to be strong. Someone has to take care
of things."

"Oh yeah? What things?"

"You. And I sent the roses, oh, because of your
blazer, because I sensed that I had offended you

earlier today, and because I wanted to open a dialogue with you."

"Ah, shit," I replied. "Just go away. The last thing I want tonight is dialogue." I poured some more Scotch down my throat and was relieved to note that my lips had become numb. In fact, I couldn't feel my face at all. About time. I stood up, realizing that with a little luck I would make it to the bedroom. Just. "Goodnight," I told her, my tongue thick. "Don't let my cats out when you leave."

The trip to the bedroom seemed interminable. I felt about as lithe as a mastodon and worse yet, my eyes kept closing, preventing me from seeing where to put my feet, each of which weighed four hundred pounds. I caromed off the wall a couple of times, and finally decided to give up. What the hell, I could sleep here, wherever here was. I was just about to ooze to the floor when someone caught me.

"Leave me alone," I whispered. "What do you want from me, anyhow? Just what the hell do you want?"

Diana wrapped her arms around me to hold me upright. "What do I want?" she whispered back. "You know the answer to that. You may be the only one who does." Then, more softly, "And you may be the only one who can give it to me."

I felt my consciousness slipping away like sand out of an opened hand, and as I fell into the viscid depths of an inky sea, I remembered something. The lines of poetry I had seen on the back of Diana's office door were from the epigraph T.S. Eliot had quoted in "The Waste Land." In a starburst of clarity, I recalled the first part, which was in Latin:

131

"Nam Sibyllam quidem Cumis ego ipse oculis meis vidi in ampulla penderea, et cum illi pueri dicerent . . ."

"And when I was in Cumae I saw with my own eyes the Sibyl, hanging in a cage, and when some boys asked her . . ."

The rest was in Greek — a question and an answer. Then I sobbed. Because I had just asked Diana the question the boys had asked of the Sibyl — the woman with the power to foretell the future, the woman who always spoke the truth. Granted one wish by the gods, the Sibyl had scooped up a handful of sand and asked to live for as many years as the grains of sand she held. But she had neglected to ask for youth. Now, old, infinitely weary, and sickened by a future that she was eternally cursed with seeing, she answered the boys truthfully. And as memory supplied the Sibyl's answer, a part of me resonated to her reply.

"Sibyl, what do you want?" the boys asked.

The Sibyl said, "I want to die."

I continued to sob, because I had it there in my hands. Diana's terrible secret, a secret she defied the world to decipher. "That's what you want, too," I whispered. "You want to die."

I was a handful of brittle leaves, carried on a cold black wind; I was a clatter of mouse bones, scrabbled from a nameless grave; I was a pair of ragged claws, scuttling across the bottom of the sea.

And then . . . and then I was a creature with legs, a lean black thing that snarled like a cougar, and I was running, running, running from the people who knew me, who wanted pieces of me. But it was useless, because behind me, as monstrous as a thunderhead, as inevitable as breathing, came my dark twin. The one who was and was not me. The one who loved the dark as I loved the light. The one who was always with me. The Dark Lady. Exhausted, I stopped, and snarling, turned to face her. But she changed her shape, melting away like smoke. Now a huge, black wave, she loomed over me and then, with a hideous roar, she fell, breaking. For one moment, I floated on her ebony breast, my face raised to the moon. Then, with a sigh that spoke my name, she began to devour me. I screamed and kicked, but she closed around my feet, holding me fast. She swallowed my legs, my hips, my heart, and in a moment I could not tell where I ended and she began.

"What do you want?" she asked me.

And then I knew. I knew how to escape it. I raised my face to the moon and howled. "I want to live," I said. With a roar of disappointment, she shuddered, then spat me out.

And I came screaming awake in my own bed.

"Jesus!" I sobbed, tears running down my face. "Will I never be free of this?"

But there was no one to answer me. I was alone. I felt suddenly, violently ill, and barely made it to the bathroom where, after what seemed like an eternity of retching, I sat on the bathroom floor, too weak to do anything but breathe. And talk to myself. So the Dark Lady had visited me again. So what? I knew what it meant: be very, very careful. Okay, I thought. I will. But careful of what? Macklin, I guessed. Fine. I'd look behind every bush, every garbage pail, every telephone pole. Caution would be my middle name. Eventually, I stood up and splashed cold water on my face. That helped. I brushed my teeth and walked back into the bedroom.

"Do you feel better?" someone asked from the hall. Diana McNeil leaned against the doorframe, hands in her pockets. I immediately felt guilty. How could I have forgotten about her?

"That's debatable," I said. "Mostly I feel like a fool." I looked at my watch. "Do you know it's three o'clock?"

"Mmhmm," she said enigmatically.

"I don't mean to sound ungrateful, but why are you still here?" A whopper of a headache had started somewhere behind my eyes and I felt hollow, disembodied. "You must have better things to do than minister to drunks. Especially drunks who try to murder you."

She eyed me from the doorway. "Why are you so hard on yourself? You made a mistake."

I felt too feeble, it was just easier to be evasive. "I lost control. I wanted to kill someone." In truth, I felt . . . soiled. Dirty. I'd been carrying around this huge desire to kill someone. It had been like a boil on my brain and was making me nuts. Well, tonight the boil burst.

"You wanted to kill someone?" she asked, her voice tight. "Who?"

"A rapist I put away when I worked at the CP's office. He got out early — some work-release rehab program. A couple nights ago he paid a visit to the woman who testified against him. I got her safely away from him so now he's coming after me. Like I told you, that's who I thought you were."

"I see," she said. Then, "I do understand."

I shook my head. "How can you? I can scarcely understand it myself." This *lust* to kill . . . It made me feel weak again, and I sat on the end of my bed.

"Listen to me," Diana said, coming to kneel beside me. "I understand exactly what you're going through. I can't talk about this easily but my . . . lover was killed about a year ago." She took a shuddering breath. Her eyes were like topaz flames. "She had been raped and beaten and left to die in a park like a gutted animal. If I could have the bastard here in front of me for just five minutes . . ." Her eyes welled with tears. "So don't tell me I don't understand, because I do." She was weeping silently now, eyes closed, the tears streaming out from under her eyelids. She made no effort to wipe them away. "I do."

I groaned. Reaching down, I gathered her and her pain into my arms. We clung to each other, two drowning sailors, tempest-tossed. "Oh Diana," I said, "killing him won't help."

"Yes, it will," she insisted, sobbing now, her head against my cheek. "It may be the only thing that will."

"No," I told her gently. "Killing won't stop the pain. That will always be there. But killing him will cost *you* something. A part of your soul. Do you want to pay that price?"

"I don't care about that," she wept hopelessly. "Not any more. I haven't cared about anything since Fran died. I know I'll never kill the bastard who did it — hell, they never even *caught* him. But that doesn't stop me wanting to kill him. And wanting to die, myself, too. God, Caitlin, I want that! I'd end my life myself, but I haven't the courage. Knives, guns, even pills — don't think I haven't thought about them. But I can't, I just can't!"

"Sshhh," I said, appalled. And then, because I was ill and tired, and it was three a.m., and Diana was weeping herself into exhaustion, I lay down on my bed, pulled her to me, and wrapped us both in my grandma's quilt. "Ssshhh," I said again, stroking her hair, because I couldn't think of anything to say. I had no words of comfort, of wisdom, of hope. There was nothing I could do for Diana McNeil. I suspected there was very little anyone could do for her. Except maybe hold her. And so I did.

Eventually she fell silent, and then she slept.

I awoke sometime before dawn to find myself alone. Too tired to try to make sense of it all, I pulled the covers around my shoulders and closed my eyes.

CHAPTER EIGHT
Friday

The day dawned as bleak and gray as my spirits. I showered, dressed in something respectable, donned my darkest sunglasses, managed a glass of water and two aspirins, poured kibble for the cats, and then somehow navigated my way through traffic to U Vic, all in a morning-after stupor. The bracing spring air revived me somewhat and I purchased a cup of coffee from one of the ubiquitous machines, pausing for a moment on one of the concrete benches in front of Emily Carr Hall before Diana's class. I didn't think I could persuade anyone of anything today, and had half a mind to go back home to bed. But then I remembered the full moon, and my promise to Perry. Groaning, I tossed the cup in a trash can.

Diana McNeil wore a mustard yellow sweater, rust colored wool pants, and oversized sunglasses. Images from the night before replayed in my mind: Diana bleeding on the floor of my pantry, Diana holding my hands, Diana sobbing against my cheek, Diana in my arms.

I walked to the front of the room. She saw me, and stopped unpacking her briefcase. "How are you?" I asked awkwardly.

"Not good," she said. "How are you?"

"About the same."

"Will you stop by my office after class? I have something to tell you, something I want you to know."

"All right," I said, then took up my post in the hall outside the classroom.

As things turned out, I may as well have stayed in bed. No one remotely resembling Tess showed up for class, and when I poked my head around the corner just before Diana's lecture began, I saw at least six empty places.

I swore under my breath, went downstairs and purchased another cardboard container of coffee, then sat on the steps of Emily Carr Hall, waiting for the sun to shine. It didn't. I realized that I had been nursing a fatuous hope that when Tess showed up for class, I'd make her see the error of her ways, silver-tongued devil that I was, and return her to the house on Beach Drive. Sure. Now I was going to have to make that awful drive up to Land's End, pry her away from her friends and protectors, wrestle her to the ground, and spirit her away. Hell, the way I felt this morning, I was fortunate to have gotten out of the house with my head attached to my body. Wrestling was definitely out. Repo could have beaten me today. I sighed, checked my watch, and went back upstairs to talk to Diana.

She was waiting in her office, back to me, looking out the window. When she heard me come in, she turned and took off her glasses. She had the beginnings of two eggplant-colored shiners, and the bridge of her nose where I had kicked her was the hue of raw hamburger. Still, she smiled, or tried to. "Why don't you close the door?" she asked.

"I can't stay long," I told her, pushing the door closed. "I have to meet someone at eleven-thirty."

She nodded. "This won't take long," she told me, her lips turning down in a rueful smile. "Maybe it isn't important, but it's something I think you ought to know. Just in case you're interested."

I waited expectantly, but she said nothing. Instead, she came very deliberately out from behind her desk and walked toward me. When I realized what she intended, it was far too late. And besides, I wasn't sure I wanted to stop her. She put one hand on my shoulder, the other at the back of my neck, and bent my head to hers. Then she kissed me.

"That's for last night," she said, her breath warm against my lips. "For listening to me."

Then she kissed me again, her lips as soft as rose petals.

"What's that for?" I asked, my voice hoarse.

"For all the wrong things," she said, caressing my cheek with the back of her hand. "For bad timing," she whispered. "For things that might have been and cannot be." She traced my eyebrows with cool fingers. I closed my eyes against the desire I felt. "Ah, Caitlin," she said in a husky voice. "I wish I had met you years ago. When I had a future."

I felt as though my heart would break, and I put my arms around her, holding her tightly to me. "We make our own futures," I told her. "Whatever you think lies ahead of you, you can turn aside from it. Your future can be whatever you choose."

She said nothing, and I knew then that anything I said would be useless. I felt a great grief begin in me then, because I knew Diana had chosen something terrible and lonely for herself. "Don't misunderstand me," she said against my cheek. "I don't want you to try to persuade me of anything. What I do want, though, well, I think you know what I want."

"Yes. I know."

She laughed a little. "I wonder. It's not entirely what you think, although part of it is that I do want to go to bed with you."

I was puzzled. "What else do you want?"

"What else? I want to know what keeps you . . . well, struggling as hard as you do. I call it 'naming the shadow.' I want you to tell me why you do it." She stepped back from me and took my hands in hers, holding them tightly. "And then I want you to do . . . something else. Will you indulge me?"

I couldn't have said no if I'd wanted to and I definitely didn't want to. I didn't care why this strange, sad, charismatic woman wanted me, but I was damned if I was going to turn her away. Things might well have turned out differently if I had, if I had let my brain, not my libido, make my decisions. I fished in my pocket for my wallet, put my spare house key into her palm, and folded her fingers around it. What she was asking me for was a very small thing, after all.

"I expect to be home sometime later today. Maybe as late as this evening."

"Thank you," she said. "I'll wait for you."

CHAPTER NINE

I found Lester sitting in a battered white Land
Rover at British Fish 'n Chips, a takeout cup of tea
in one hand, an issue of the campus paper in the
other. He looked disgustingly young and alert, jeans
and blue chambray shirt freshly pressed, sandy hair
clean and neatly combed, complexion ruddy, blue
eyes bright. He took one look at me, though, and his
eyes widened in surprise behind his aviator glasses.
"Caitlin, what . . ."
"No jokes this morning, kiddo," I told him. "I feel

six times as bad as I look." I parked my MG and climbed into the Land Rover. "Just drive," I told him, slumping down in my seat. "Wake me up when we get to that yuppie restaurant by the ferry dock. Tidal Raves or something like that. I'll be ready for breakfast then. Or lunch. Right now, though, if I don't close my eyes, I'll expire."

Wise youth, he just nodded and drove.

After a snooze, and a lunch comprised of chicken noodle soup, toast, and weak tea, I felt as though I might be able to cope with the day. Lester watched me anxiously as I ate, but refrained from asking any questions.

"Okay," I said, leaning back in my chair and pouring my second cup of tea. "I think I might live."

He relaxed visibly. "Gosh, Caitlin, I was worried."

I fixed him with a stern look. "Let it be a lesson to you, buster. Late-night drinking binges are hell on productivity. When you get to be a famous journalist, take my advice and stick to Red Zinger if you want to see your byline."

He nodded agreement. "I tried drinking once," he confided. "Gin with 7-Up chasers." My chicken noodle soup gave a queasy lurch in my gut. "My roommate and I polished off a whole bottle of Tanqueray one night," Lester continued. "I was so sick the next day I couldn't even blink without wanting to throw up. I've never drunk anything since then. Not even beer. I nurse ginger ale at parties. But don't spread it around, okay?"

I smiled. "Your secret is safe with me."

"So, like, why do you *really* need to go up to Land's End?" he asked.

I saw no harm in telling him part of the truth. "It's this case I'm working on. My employer's missing sister is supposedly living up there on one of the old estates. It belongs to a guy named Crowley but apparently the property manager is renting it out and pocketing the money. I don't care about that, though — I'm not working for him. I'm just supposed to talk the sister into coming home."

"Oh. How will you do that?"

I shrugged. "Beats me. Something will occur to me though. That's why we PIs are so highly paid."

He nodded. "Because you're so persuasive, right?"

"Wrong. We can command the stunning fees we do because we're so inventive, kiddo. Terminally right-brained. When Plan A doesn't work, we can invent B, C, and D at the drop of a hat. We're masters, or mistresses if you will, of the extemporaneous. Heck, we can always think of *something*. It comes from being English majors in college."

"I see," he said doubtfully. Poor Lester, he never knows when I'm pulling his leg. It's just as well. It keeps him guessing.

"Okay, here's the drill," I told him. "We'll ask directions to Crowley's place at the gas station, then drive on up there and park. You'll shoot a few pictures while I poke around. We're not going to be surprised to find the place occupied because no one tells us nothin' anyway. We're just paid flunkies."

"Got it."

"I have an extensive form to fill out," I explained. "So I'll have to look at, gosh, just about everything."

He grinned, getting into the spirit of things. "And you'll have to talk to everyone there. To find out what repairs are needed before the real estate company can put a price on the place."

"Not bad," I congratulated him. "For a left-brained journalist, not bad at all."

We parked around the side of the Land's End Deli-Mart, out of sight of the nosy kid, and I sent Lester in to try his luck. When he didn't return immediately, I began to feel optimistic. Obviously his masculine charm was working wonders on her. Who knows what tasty tidbits he was gleaning along with directions? He emerged finally, a paper bag in his hand, a dazed expression on his face.

"Hey, what happened in there?" I asked him.

"Oh, nothing," he said, blushing furiously. "She's rather, well, forward, isn't she?"

"That she is. What's in the bag?"

"Crackers. And a bottle of club soda. I thought your stomach might appreciate them."

"Thanks, Lester," I said, genuinely touched. "So, did she tell you how to get to Crowley's?"

He backed the Land Rover out of its parking place and navigated onto Land's End Road. "Yeah. And a lot of things I didn't want to know, too."

I patted his arm. "Ain't real life grand? Just consider it part of your journalistic training. Mingling with the masses."

He looked ill.

"Kinda makes the camera store look more attractive, doesn't it?"

"Lester Baines, shopkeeper," he groaned. "What a waste of four years of college. And what do I tell my mother? She's paid for half my tuition. She thinks I'm going to be a reporter."

"Hey, take it easy," I told him. "Your mom will probably jump for joy. Who wants her kid out pounding the pavement chasing stories when he could have a cushy job as the manager of a thriving business?"

"Well . . ."

"Apart from seeing your byline, what's so great about journalism, anyhow? What do you like about it?"

He thought for a couple of moments. "You know, what really appeals to me is the production end," he said. "Design. Layout and pasteup. Graphics. Making things look good. I got a chance to use some desktop publishing software recently, and it knocked me out! That's where the future is for small publications."

"Well," I said, "why can't you design and write a newsletter for the camera shop clients? Educate them about how to take good pictures, how to use their video equipment? That kind of thing."

He looked at me hopefully. "Hey, I could do that, couldn't I? But still . . ." He trailed off mournfully.

"Just think it over," I said. "Keep your options open. Maybe you ought to call your mom and talk things over with her."

He shook his head firmly. "No. She'd only worry about me." He set his jaw stubbornly. "You know what she does for a living? She's a janitor. She cleans offices at night. Then, to put *me* through school, my mom cleans rich people's houses during the day. She scrubs *toilets,* Caitlin."

"She must love you a lot," I said quietly.

He nodded. "She does. I know that. When I was at home, I always had a job — delivering papers, cutting lawns, that sort of thing. *I* always helped *her.* I never even mentioned the fact that I wanted to go to college because I knew it was out of the question. She wouldn't let me get a student loan, and you know scholarships are as scarce as hen's teeth in Canada. So she made me a deal — she'd pay half if I paid half." He shook his head. "Every month, she sends me two hundred and forty dollars. I put my two-forty with it and trot over to the accounting office. Eight months a year, for nearly four years now. That's what has me worried. If I take this camera shop thing, will she —"

"Will she think she's gotten her money's worth?" I guessed.

"Yeah. That's it."

"I don't know, kiddo. All I know is that it's your life, your future. I'm sure your mom would want you to make a choice you're comfortable with. And only you can do that."

"I know," he said gloomily. "Well, let's look on the bright side. Maybe Mr. Henderson will recover. Or maybe a long-lost child will appear to contest the will. Or a niece. Anyone. Nuts," he said after a moment's silence. "Is this what being a responsible adult is all about? All these . . . choices?"

"Yup," I assured him. "All those choices. To do or not to do. To be or not to be."

"Nuts," he repeated. "You know, sometimes I

wish I were ten years old again. That was the best summer of my life. Mom rented a cabin on a lake for two whole weeks. We used to get up early when it was dark and row out to the reeds to fish. Then we'd wait for the sun to come up and we'd have a breakfast picnic — tea from a thermos, and scones. We usually caught a few fish, but Mom would throw them back. Too small, she always said. After a few hours, we'd go back to the cabin, and have some real breakfast — bacon and eggs and toast and jam and more tea. Gallons of tea. Then I'd explore, and catch tadpoles, and swim and Mom would read." He shrugged. "Sounds dumb, doesn't it? But I'd give anything to be that kid again for just one day."

"It doesn't sound dumb." I sensed I'd better tread carefully. "And you'll carry that memory with you forever. But being an adult means having the freedom and the ability to make new memories for ourselves, memories that will be every bit as precious as the ones of our childhood. We have the power to make our lives what we want, Lester," I told him earnestly, "to choose beauty and kindness and love over ugliness and rancor and poverty of spirit. That's what being an adult really means. It means . . . well, freedom. Freedom to choose. And, as you said, the choices are sometimes hard." I shut up, feeling foolish. Hell, Lester didn't need a speech from me.

"I never knew you felt that way," he said after a moment. "Thanks for telling me. And thanks for listening to me, too. Boy, you must think I'm some kind of jerk."

"Is that what you think I am?" I smiled.

"You? Of course not!"

"Well then, why should I think that of you?"

"Oh, well . . ."

"Drive, Mr. Baines. Just drive." I pointed to the road ahead. "'This is the forest primeval, the murmuring pines and the hemlocks,'" I quoted. "Do you know who said that?"

"Er, gee, no I don't," he said, sounding worried.

"Longfellow," I told him. "It's from *Evangeline*. But don't fret," I teased, "I won't let your mom know you weren't paying attention in poetry class. Just try not to hit every pit and chasm in the road, please."

Smiling sheepishly, he adjusted his glasses and drove.

After an eternity of lurching and bounding over, into, and out of the craters and ruts of Land's End Road, we were suddenly there — the entrance to the forested estates of the privileged. Lester idled the engine and referred to his notes while I looked around. Two immense fieldstone pillars flanked a narrow road through the trees, and between the pillars stretched an iron arch, now badly rusted, that must have once borne a sign of some kind.

"Through the pillars and straight on for half a mile," Lester said. "Then when we pass a green mailbox, we take the third turn on the right."

We drove slowly down the narrow road, Lester watching the odometer. On my side of the road, I could dimly make out the shapes of immense dwellings, crouching like strange humped beasts in the green gloom. Here and there through the trees, I could see the glint of sunlight on water, and I realized that each of the estates had the ocean as its back yard.

"Spooky," Lester commented.

"Yeah," I agreed. "Hard to believe they're all deserted now."

"Here's the mailbox," Lester said. "Now we need to watch for the third turnoff."

No one could have missed the turnoff because the way was barred by a locked gate. I hopped out to investigate, kneeling to examine the shiny new chain and padlock, when a voice called from a copse of cedars to my right.

"Hey, this is private property. Just turn around and drive on back to town."

A small, curly-haired blonde in jeans and hiking boots walked out of the bushes, hands in the pockets of a red down vest. I recognized her immediately: the driver of the Bronco.

"Nope," I said pleasantly, straightening up and smiling. "Can't do that."

"Oh? Why not? Lost your way?" she asked, one foot on the gate's bottom rail.

"Nope," I repeated. "We're from Island Realty. Apparently the owner is going to put this place on the market. We need to make a pre-appraisal report before Island can put a price on it." I wrinkled my brow for maximum effect. "You know, the real estate company didn't say anything about tenants. They did mention a caretaker, though. Are you she? A Ms. Jubal, I believe?" I raised an eyebrow.

Clearly flustered, she stood indecisively in the middle of the road. "Er, well, no. She's back at the house. And we're not exactly tenants. We're just . . . staying here." She frowned, clearly thinking hard.

150

"Ah," I said. "Well, whatever. My associate and I *do* need to get in, though. We won't be long. A few pictures —"

"Pictures?" she squeaked, aghast.

"Well, yes. To document any damage, as well as one good shot for the newspaper ad."

"I'll get Callie. Wait here," she said, and fled down the road.

"Quick thinking," Lester commented when I returned to the Land Rover.

"Darned right," I agreed. "Like I told you, PIs are ever resourceful."

"Say, did you really major in English?"

"Yup. With a minor in philosophy. I'm happy to say my education rendered me totally unable to take my place as a productive member of society."

"Meaning?"

"Meaning it was great fun, but I graduated not being able to *do* a goddamned thing."

"Hard on the bank account."

"Harder still on the ego."

"So what did you do?"

"What everyone else does who has a liberal education and no marketable skills. I taught school."

"Oh."

"Heads up," I told him. "Here comes the larcenous caretaker."

A sturdy-looking, ruddy-cheeked young woman with very short brown hair, no-nonsense jeans, and a wary expression strode up to us. "I'm Callie Jubal, Mr. Crowley's caretaker," she said in a distinctly unfriendly tone. She stuck her hands in the pockets of a denim jacket and glared at us. "Can I help you?"

151

I fixed her with a reproachful look. Brazen hussy. "Yes, you can. You can unlock this gate so my associate and I can come in and do our job." I sniffed for emphasis. "They didn't tell us at Island Realty that we'd have this much trouble."

To her credit, she didn't budge. "Crowley didn't tell me he intended to sell."

"Oh? When did you last speak with him?"

"I don't know. Sometime last month —"

"Well, that's the problem, then!" I exclaimed. "I talked with him yesterday."

"Oh," she replied, clearly surprised.

"He spoke very highly of you," I assured her. "Mentioned how reliable and trustworthy you were. He's very pleased with your work."

She blushed to the roots of her hair. "Shit," she muttered. Then, "How long will all this take?"

"Oh, an hour or so. Maybe less."

"Okay," she said, dragging a key from the depths of one pocket. She unlocked the gate and swung it open. "Tell him to drive through," she called. "I want to lock up after him."

I waved Lester in and Callie swung the gate closed. "Listen," she told me once she'd snapped the padlock shut, "there are some people staying at the estate. Friends of mine." She sighed. "Crowley doesn't know about them."

"Oh," I replied, pretending to digest this information. "Well, he won't find out about it from me," I said with a conspiratorial wink.

"Thanks," she muttered. "What about him?"

"He works for me," I said. "All he does is take pictures. He wouldn't care if there was a tribe of Hottentots living there. Don't worry."

"I owe you for this," she said.

"No problem," I said breezily. "Let's get started. The sooner we begin, the sooner we'll be gone."

That prompted a small smile from the dour Callie. "Okay," she said. "This way."

Crowley's estate occupied about two acres of prime forest land, and I suppose in its heyday it had been quite a place. Once we got in past the thick fringe of firs that hid the estate from the road, the forest thinned out and the claustrophobic feeling I'd had vanished. Now I could see — up through the branches of the occasional fir to the powder-blue sky, and out past the estate to the jade-colored waters of the bay beyond. We parked in a pool of dappled sun and shadow and walked toward the massive covered front porch. A bluejay kibitzed noisily from the top of a young pine, and in the distance, we heard the eerie cry of a loon. Apart from bird calls, there was absolute silence.

"It's like being in church," Lester commented, looking awed. "What a place."

Callie waited for us on the porch. "Go ahead in," she said. "I've talked to the others and they're going on down to the water for a while. So you won't be bothered by anyone while you look around." She put her hands in her pockets and eyed me curiously. "What do you need to do, anyhow?"

"Oh, you know, measure the rooms, make a note of the mod cons, count the fireplaces and closets — that sort of thing. And check to see that everything is in working order."

"What about him?" she asked, inclining her head in Lester's direction. "Does he really have to go in?"

I raised an eyebrow. "Well, yes he does. We need a couple of interior shots as well as some exterior ones."

"Oh all right," she said testily. "It's just that we don't like men a whole lot."

"I'll do my best to keep him under control," I said.

She glowered at Lester, flared her nostrils, then stomped off to join her friends down by the water.

"Whew," Lester said. "What a woman. Are the rest of them just as friendly?"

"Probably," I said, pushing the front door open.

"What did she mean about them not liking men?"

"Just what she said, I suppose."

"Then, does that mean they like, er, well —"

"Women? Maybe. Or maybe they don't like anyone." I was only half-listening to Lester, my mind somewhere else. Julia Springer had told me that she and Tess had gone out with a couple of basketball players over the Christmas holidays. Yet here was Tess, living with a bunch of lesbian separatists. It didn't make sense. Hmmm. Perhaps I ought to talk to Julia again. "Wander around down here and take a couple of pictures," I told Lester. "I'll be upstairs."

"Are you looking for something in particular?" he asked, unpacking his camera. "If I knew what it was, I could help."

I shook my head. "Thanks, but I don't know myself. I'd like to have a conversation with the missing sister. Apart from that, I'll just play it by ear." I had already decided not to tell Lester anything about the Daughters of Artemis. What he didn't know couldn't get him into trouble.

A flight of wide carpeted stairs led up to a large landing lined with bookcases, all full. A bull's-eye window gave the miniature library some light, and as I trudged to the top of the stairs, I could see quite a number of rooms opening onto the hall. The house smelled musty up here — the books and the old-fashioned flowered carpet, I guessed. I fought a sneeze and wondered if this place had central heating. Probably not. I'd noticed a massive fieldstone fireplace in the living room downstairs, and that might well be the only source of heat the house possessed. After all, even Victoria's very well-to-do wouldn't have wanted to come up here in the wintertime. I could sympathize with them — winter on a Pacific Northwest inlet wasn't my idea of paradise, either.

What I had told Lester about not knowing what I was looking for was only partly true. I had some idea — anything pertaining to the Daughters. A vague plan had been forming in my mind. If I could discover specifically what they were up to, I might be able to blackmail them, or use the information to pry Tess away from them.

I wandered down the hall, poking my head into open doorways, but the rooms seemed unused. One at the end of the hall, however, was different. It looked like a room in the women's dorm at college — desks piled high with books and notepads, clothes thrown over chairs. Several single beds had evidently been pulled into the room from somewhere else, and I guessed this was a communal sleeping room. One

glance at the corner of the room told me why —
another fieldstone fireplace. Presumably this one
shared the same flue as the massive fireplace
downstairs. So it was probably pretty warm in here
when the downstairs fireplace was in use. I poked
around in the piles of books and papers on the
desks, and stirred the clothes around a little, but
uncovered nothing of interest.

I walked back out into the hall and stood there
for a moment, hands on hips, uncertain of what to
do next. Evidently the Daughters of Artemis weren't
advertising their plans on a flow chart taped to the
wall. Pity. I was going to have to do some real
detecting.

For that matter, where *did* they concoct their
plans? Where was their "deep, vaulted cell" in which,
like Purcell's witches, they prepared their charms?

"Hey, Lester," I called from the stairs, "do you
see a basement door down there?"

A faint reply came from the kitchen. "Yeah, I
think so."

Heartened, I crossed the cavernous living room,
picking my way through the shrouded shapes of
sofas, tables, and chairs. One sofa had been
uncovered, and now sat sensibly close to the
fireplace. I bet the Daughters burned a lot of wood
just keeping the chill off.

Lester met me in the kitchen. "Big place," he
said, blowing his nose. "Cold, too. I think the door to
the basement's over there. It's locked, though."

I rattled the handle — an old-fashioned glass
knob. Sure enough, it was locked. "Look at the
keyhole," I said.

Lester bent over and peered at the door. "What about it?"

"It uses a skeleton key, for God's sake!" I told him. "I haven't seen one of those in years."

"Hard to pick?"

"Yeah." I crouched down and squinted through the keyhole. "Oho — the key's been left in the lock. See if you can find a knife, kiddo. One with a skinny blade."

Lester was back in a flash, a steak knife in his hand. "What are you going to do?" he whispered.

"Watch." I took a folded newspaper from a stack by the basement door, unfolded a couple of pages, and slid them under the door. Then I took Lester's steak knife, inserted it into the keyhole, and wiggled. The key fell out of the lock and landed with a *tink* on the paper on the other side of the door. Gingerly I pulled the paper toward me and there, reposing in the midst of the classified ads, was the skeleton key. "*Voila,*" I said, standing up and unlocking the door.

"Hey!" he commented.

I put the key back in the lock on the inside of the door and reached around for the light switch. Then I realized I wouldn't need it for there was a light burning at the bottom of the stairs.

"Carry on taking pictures," I told him. "I'll just take a quick look around down here."

As his footsteps retreated across the kitchen, I took a deep breath and began to descend the cellar stairs. Halfway down I paused, realizing with a twinge of annoyance that I was dragging my feet. Delaying. What was going on here? *Oh, for heaven's sake,* I muttered. *It's only a basement. And a rather well-lighted one at that. Get a grip, Reece.* Disgusted with such wimpishness, I strode purposefully down the stairs, feeling inordinately pleased with myself when I finally stood at the bottom.

Downstairs turned out to be nothing more ominous than an area half as large as the main floor, divided into a series of small rooms, neatly partitioned off with plywood and two-by-fours. One room was a walk-in wine cellar, but the dusty racks held nothing but cobwebs. Another was a storeroom stacked with lawn furniture and outdoor game equipment. I recognized dusty croquet hoops and mallets, and a badminton net folded in one corner. The third and last room, however, was a puzzle. It was brightly lit, and contained a table in the middle of the room, and a series of glass-fronted cabinets reminiscent of lawyers' bookcases along one wall.

I went over and peered into one of the cabinets. A pile of white towels, bottles of Betadine and alcohol, gauze, tape, surgical instruments. What was this — a makeshift clinic? A video camera, VCR, and television monitor sat on a wheeled rack against the back wall, a pile of tapes on the rack's bottom shelf. Curiouser and curiouser. A bulletin board on the wall behind the video rack held a 24 x 36 red posterboard with a series of photographs taped to it and names printed underneath the photos in black magic marker. I had just grabbed the rack to move it out of the way when a voice called from behind me.

"Hey, who are you, and what the hell do you think you're doing?"

I turned. It was Tess. She didn't look a whole lot like the kid in the photo, but it was still her, freckle-faced and blue-eyed. Her hair was a lot shorter and a lot dirtier and, just as Julia had remarked, her haberdashery left a lot to be desired. The brown-and-white checked flannel shirt was rolled up well above the elbows, revealing a turtleneck that must have once been a rather pretty blue. Now it was in an advanced state of grubbiness — the cuffs alone would have made my grandma turn pale. Her jeans sported dried mud on the knees and her boots were a sight. I frowned, wondering what had brought about this change from a pretty, well-groomed teenager to this slovenly, unwashed harridan.

I hesitated. It had taken me ages to find this kid. What was I to do — continue my realtor charade? Be truthful and risk having her bolt on me? Ah, hell, I decided abruptly, why not go for it?

"I'm a private investigator," I told her. "My name is Caitlin Reece. Your sister sent me to bring you home."

She flicked a quick glance at the stairs, decided she could get there before me, and delivered what she clearly thought was an effective parting shot.

"You can tell her to go to hell."

My patience snapped. "I won't tell her anything of the sort," I said, feeling my blood start to boil. "She's worried about you, Miss Smart Mouth, but the kid I see standing here isn't worth worrying about. Julia's worried about you, too, but I guess you'd like me to communicate the same message to her. No luck, Tootsie. You know what I'm going to do instead? I'm going to tell them to forget you. You're not worth worrying about."

To my surprise, her lower lip started to tremble. "What do you know about it?" she wailed. "What do any of you know?"

I decided to push her a little further. "Beats me. If I had to guess, though, I'd say you're suffering from an inflated conviction of your own self-importance. Terminal teenage angst." I made myself sneer a little. "My God, how tedious. Grow up, Tess. If you'd paid attention in science class, you'd have learned that the world revolves around the sun, not around you." Harsh words, but from my fleeting impression of Tess, words that just might work.

Tess exploded. "You ignorant *fuck!* You're just like all the rest of them — my sister, Julia, all of them! You don't know anything!"

"Oh, and your new friends do, right? What are you all doing up here anyhow — holding each other's hands while you piss and moan about how unfair life is? What is it this time? Job discrimination, world hunger, the ozone layer, the whales?"

She stood with her eyes closed, fists clenched at her sides, tears flowing freely down her face. I felt like a worm.

I continued relentlessly. "No? Well maybe it's the high cost of housing, or the rain forests, or the homeless, or the starving children in Appalachia, or —"

"Stop it!" she screamed. "How can you just *say* those things? You and my sister and Julia and all

160

the other middle-class bitches who've never known one minute's suffering. Well, I hate you — I hate all of you!"

"Oh, it's suffering we're talking about is it? Well, what have you and the other members of your club suffered?" I scoffed, aware that I was pushing her dangerously close to the edge. "You get your VISA applications turned down?"

"You shithead," she sobbed. "We've all been *raped!* That's what we share, and that's what Julia didn't want to hear, that's what Perry would never understand. My big, tough, strong sister — can you see someone trying to rape her? Jesus, she'd kill them! And she'd never believe I tried, but *I couldn't stop him!*" She threw back her head and howled, "I would have killed him, I would have, but I wasn't strong enough!" She struck herself on the shoulder with one clenched fist. "God, how I hate this body, this weak, *woman's* body. I hate it!"

I took several steps toward her, reaching for her, wanting to comfort her, but she misinterpreted my actions. She swung a fist blindly as she ran past me, and it connected with the side of my head, knocking me off balance for just a moment. When I turned, she was halfway up the stairs. I sprinted after her. "Dammit, Tess," I yelled. "Let me help you! Tell me who the bastard was!"

"Ask Julia," she sobbed, scrabbling up the stairs and into the kitchen.

I was right behind her. "Tess, wait! He doesn't have to get away with this. We can go and pick him up. Now. This afternoon. Let the police deal with him."

"Fuck off," she cried. "*We're* going to deal with

161

him." The kitchen door slammed shut behind her as she ran down the path to the dock. Oh goody. Now all the girls would know about my little charade.

"Ah, shit," I said to the empty kitchen and ran after her.

"What did you say to Tess?" Callie demanded as I pounded down the planks of the dock toward her. "Did you upset her?"

"Guess so," I said, watching Tess try to start the motor of a little Zodiac she had pushed off the rocky beach into the bay. So she hadn't told Callie about my duplicity. Well, maybe she'd been too upset to talk to anyone. Good job, Reece, I congratulated myself. You bullied her until she cut and ran. And that worried me a great deal. The open sea in a little rubber boat was no place for someone who had her mind on other things. Drownings happened that way.

"Tess!" Callie yelled. "Come on back!"

But Tess showed no indication that she had heard. Instead, she stood up in the boat, put one foot on the motor, gave a great heave on the starting cord . . . and fell overboard.

"Tess!" Callie screamed. By this time the three other women who were living at Crowley's had come running and we all stood on the dock watching Tess flounder in the water, about a hundred feet from us.

"We have to do something!" Callie shrieked. I looked around. Two of the women were standing open-mouthed in horror, and the third was weeping.

"Ah, shit," I exclaimed for the second time that

162

day. Shedding my jacket and sneakers, I ran to the end of the dock and, trying very hard not to think about what I was doing, hit the water in a racing dive.

As the icy water closed over me, I thought my heart would stop. I felt as though my body had become an arrow of ice, a shaft of burning cold, and for one panic-stricken moment as I lifted my head, I was unable to breathe. Then I regained control of my muscles, and my lungs, and gasped as I drew breath.

"Jesus Christ!" I yelled as I set out in the fastest crawl I could manage. A dozen strokes brought me to Tess and as I straightened up to tread water, she went under again. But this time she didn't come up. I could see the pale blur of her face under the surface and without thinking, I tucked my body and dove for her. As I opened my eyes in the murky jade-colored depths, I knew that I had very little strength left. The cold water was weakening me, sapping my energy until I felt that every move was like pushing my way through molasses. Worst of all, I knew that if I couldn't grab Tess on this try, I wouldn't get another. I just didn't have the strength. I straightened my body, and kicked, hands outstretched, reaching for the collar of her plaid shirt. But it slipped through my fingers.

I twisted my body, reaching, reaching . . . and my hand fastened on her hair. I hung on, dragging Tess to me until I was able to let go of her hair and get a good grip on her collar. Then I put an arm around her chest, hugged her to me, and kicked for the surface. There was only one problem: my kick had no oomph. I hung there, suspended between heaven and earth, feeling that I would be here forever. I raised my head to look at the surface but it seemed impossibly far away, a pewter coffin lid. A voice somewhere in the back of my mind urged me to move, kick, thrash, twitch, anything, but it all seemed like too much effort. The tightness in my chest told me that in another moment I would have to breathe, but the thought of filling my lungs with icy water seemed strangely welcome. You're going to die, you fool, I told myself, and as I hung there, I had a sudden vision of the Sybil of Cumae, hanging in her cage, suspended forever between heaven and earth, life and death. "I want to die," she had said. Well, I could understand that. Life was definitely not all it was cracked up to be, and an eternity of it would be far too much to bear. Still, I decided, I might like to bear it a little longer.

I tried to imagine what my breath would look like as it rose to the surface — a flurry of bright bubbles, a school of shiny-sided minnows, a handful of tossed silver coins. Bemused, I had almost decided to exhale and see for myself when the surface of the water was shattered above me. A hand reached out of the quicksilver heavens, and I was more than a little confused. What was this, the hand of the Goddess? And what did it want with me? Maybe this was a latter-day feminist version of Michaelangelo's Creation. Oh, what the heck, I thought, why not play Adam and touch the Goddess's hand? So I raised my hand to grab the celestial fingers only to feel my own hand seized and my arm yanked nearly out of its socket.

"Gaaak," I yelled, as my head broke the surface

of the water and I gasped for air. "You're ripping my arm off!"

Someone grabbed me, and I felt arms trying to haul me over the rubber sides of a Zodiac.

"For God's sake, take Tess," I said, gagging and retching as my nose sank below the surface again. I turned and gave Tess a shove. Two pairs of arms took her from me and hauled her into the boat. Then they reached for me. One belonged to Lester, I saw, and one to Callie.

"Someone breathe for Tess," I said, my teeth chattering as they helped me aboard. Another woman had wrapped Tess in a blanket and was working on her, pinching her nose and breathing into her mouth. Everything seemed under control.

"Good," I said, through lips that had grown too numb to speak. "Real good." Then I passed out.

When I came around, the first thing I saw was flames. *I'm in hell,* I thought. *It's finally happened. I didn't go to heaven, I led too rotten a life. Now I'll have to spend eternity atoning for my transgressions. What a bummer.* Then I opened my eyes a little wider and saw Lester, clad in a hot pink sweatshirt and a green parka.

"Hi," he said. "How are you?"

"I'm not sure," I said wearily. "At first I thought I must be dead, but now I see how cute you look, I'm not sure. Where are your clothes?"

"Same place yours are," he told me. "In the kitchen, drying out."

I looked down. I was wrapped in a sleeping bag

and a little exploration told me that someone had dressed me in sweats before popping me in. I felt like a wiener in a hot dog bun. As the memory of my little swim came back to me, I shuddered violently. "Tess?"

"She's okay," Lester said, pointing to a sleeping bag on the other couch. "She started breathing right away, answered questions, knew who she was and all that. Callie made hot tea and we poured gallons of it into her. She's sleeping now."

My teeth had begun to chatter. "Say, Lester, thanks," I said. "I was sure glad to see that arm coming toward me. I just couldn't kick to the surface. You probably saved both me and Tess, you know."

He blushed as pink as his sweatshirt and adjusted his glasses fussily. "Er, um, no problem."

I smiled. "Got any more of that tea around?"

"Sure," he said, leaping off the couch.

"Wait a second. What do Callie and the others know? Did you tell them why we were really here?"

He looked proud of himself. "Nope. Not a word. They wondered why Tess took off in the boat, but I didn't tell them a thing. Neither did she. So it's up to you, I guess."

"What's up to her?" Callie demanded as she came through the little aisle between the two couches.

I sighed. "It's up to me to decide whether we ought to tell you the truth or not. I guess we ought to." I gave Lester a meaningful look and he disappeared into the kitchen.

Callie sat down on the couch by Tess's feet. She didn't seem particularly upset. "Go on."

"I'm a private detective," I told her. "I was hired by Tess's sister to find her and bring her home."

Callie grimaced. "I guessed it was something like that," she said resignedly.

I raised an eyebrow. "Oh?"

"Yeah. People like Tess, they just can't disappear. I tried to tell that to Gillian, but she wouldn't listen. She thought it was a really good idea to stash her up here." She grimaced again. "But then, no one can tell Gillian anything. Except maybe Diana."

I nodded, hoping Callie would continue. "Gillian does seem rather, well, forceful."

Callie shrugged. "She gets things done. I don't agree with her methods, but then they're none of my business. I'm not really one of the Daughters anyhow." She smiled a little sadly. "I'm just one of Gillian's old lovers."

And good old Gillian, if I wasn't mistaken, had eyes for only Diana. Poor Callie. "Aren't you worried that Crowley might find out you're letting people live here?"

"Nope. He hasn't set foot up here in years. My dad used to manage the property, but he's an alcoholic now so he can't do much. I send Crowley the reports, and bills for any repairs I make, and he sends money." She gave me a sidelong glance. "If you're asking me don't I know it's wrong, of course I do. But I couldn't . . . say no to Gillian. Once she found out about this place, there was no peace until she saw it. And once she'd seen it, she and the others moved in."

"The others — those are the three women who were on the dock?"

"Yeah."

And as much as I hated to ask the next question, I had to know the answer. "And Diana McNeil. Right?"

"Well, yes and no," Callie said.

I was surprised to find how relieved I was. "What do you mean?"

"Well, Diana knows that Gillian formed this group called the Daughters of Artemis. She knows they escort women from classes to their cars and so on. She even laughed about the name."

"The name?"

"Yeah. Artemis is the Greek version of the goddess Diana. Get it?"

"I get it." Belatedly. Sometimes my stupidity amazes even me. The Daughters of Artemis indeed. Give me a break! If I had had my wits about me, I could have saved myself this little jaunt up to Land's End. Instead of playing bedtime games with Diana, I could have pursued more fruitful endeavors. "Let's get back to yes and no," I continued. "Are you telling me that Diana knew about the group's on-campus activities but was ignorant of what else they were planning?"

"I'm pretty sure that's right," Callie said. "Gillian used to talk a lot about presenting Diana with a *fait accompli*, something daring, something that would make Diana see Gillian as a warrior."

"I'm not following this. A warrior?"

"Yeah. That's one of the classifications Diana makes in her book — one of the stages that women have to pass through on their way to wholeness. The warrior is the second-last stage of the journey."

Ye gods. "Just for my own information, what's the last?"

Callie wrinkled her brow. "Diana calls it the alchemist. One who has the power to transform others and to name the shadow." The hair rose on the back of my neck. Naming the shadow — wasn't that what Diana had said she wanted to talk to me about tonight? Weirder and weirder. With difficulty, I wrenched my mind back to the present.

"So you think Diana isn't involved in this. Except in name."

"That's what I think," Callie said. "I could be wrong, though. Gillian *could* have told her all about it. But I don't think so. Gillian wants to do something brave and imaginative. Something she thinks Diana will approve of."

"Jesus, Callie, no one in her right mind would approve of her students committing crimes."

Callie nodded. "I know. But Gillian and Ruth, they're pretty militant. They're determined to do something to make men suffer. You know, an eye for an eye." She looked at me abruptly. "Speaking of that, you'd better go. Ruth and the others have gone into town to get Gillian." She snorted a little. "They told me to keep you here until she comes. But don't worry, I won't."

"Thanks," I said, wondering just how she had intended to restrain me. A lasso? On second thought, the shape I was in, a three-year-old could have held me down.

"Your clothes are dry," she offered.

"I'll go put them on in a minute. But right now, there's something I need to be sure about. What is it the Daughters intend to do? Can you tell me? Don't misunderstand me — the only reason I want to know is to keep Tess out of it."

She nodded. "I figured that, too. But you can't. Tess is in too deep. She's obsessed with this. She's found something that makes her life make sense again. There's no way she'll turn back now."

I persisted because I had to be sure. "What, Callie? What can't she turn away from?"

Callie looked up at me, a panicked look in her eyes. "The Daughters — Gillian and the others — they're going to . . ." She trailed off. "Jesus, I can't say it."

"Let me," I offered. I thought of the table downstairs and the rudimentary surgical supplies I had seen in the cupboard. "They're going to kidnap some poor schmuck and castrate him. Isn't that right?"

She nodded.

"Callie, they'll kill him."

"Maybe not. One of the other women — Ellie — used to work in a vet's office. She's assisted at lots of castrations. She says men are no different from cats and dogs except for having bigger balls. Castration isn't exactly a life-threatening procedure. Pets recover from it in hours."

I sat up and threw the sleeping bag off my legs. "These women will be committing about five different crimes, most of them felonies. Don't they care?"

Callie shrugged. "They have strong feelings about rapists. They've all been raped — that's what drew them together."

I groaned. Of course. Artemis the chaste. Artemis the goddess of virgins. But Artemis the huntress, too. A huntress who had turned her dogs on poor Actaeon and harried him to his death for daring to sneak a peek at her while she was bathing. I was disgusted with myself. What was the point of a classical education if I was becoming too feeble-minded to make use of it?

Callie continued, "And the fact that the Full Moon Rapist is still free and walking around after three attacks is more than they can take. The campus cops kind of treat rape as a joke, and the Metro police haven't exactly given it priority."

I knew all too well what she was talking about. At the CP's office we had to let several campus rapists plead to lesser charges for lack of a good case. In a black mood, I put on my salt-stiffened clothes, then joined Lester in the Land Rover.

We found a phone booth on the highway and I dialed Julia Springer's number, not really expecting her to be in. To my surprise, she was.

"Julia, it's Caitlin Reece. I need to talk to you."

"You found Tess, didn't you?" she asked, a catch in her voice.

"I did. And now I need to talk to you."

Silence.

I gritted my teeth. "Don't do this for me, Julia. Do it for Tess."

"But she made me promise not to tell," Julia said, sounding about six years old.

"I can imagine she did. But the time for silence is over. We need to work together now, and I need you to tell me the truth."

Again, silence.

"C'mon, Julia. I know Tess was raped, and I know that's why she ran away. Let's try to help her. Taking revenge by castrating her rapist isn't going to solve anything."

"I know that," she said. "And I guess I knew all along that's what she wanted to do. I just didn't want to admit it to myself. All right, I'll talk to you."

"Give me an hour. Then meet me at The Blethering Place. Don't change your mind, Julia. There's a lot at stake here."

"I won't change my mind. I'll be there."

I was so tired I could hardly stand up. But I fished another twenty cents out of the depths of my pocket and dialed Sandy's number. To my infinite relief, he answered at once.

"Don't say anything," I said. "Just listen. I'm going to meet a kid in about an hour at The Blethering Place. Unless I'm wrong, she's going to give me the identity of a rapist. I'd like you to be sitting at a nearby table so that when we're done, I can just hand her over to you. I really think you ought to talk to this guy. The rape occurred around Christmas, and I have a feeling . . ." I paused. Sandy was one of the few people I didn't have to beat around the bush with. He knew that quite a few of my "feelings" had panned out. "Well, the time frame and the place are both right. Coincidences like that bother me."

"Sweet Jesus," Sandy breathed.

"Let's just say that if it turns out the perp isn't your guy, he's still a rapist and needs to be picked up. Whaddya say?"

"An hour from now at The Blethering Place? I'll be there. With bells on."

"Good," I said wearily. "Real good."

I knew I had to drag my body home and hit the shower before I saw Julia, but I had one last call to make. Through the glass of the phone booth I could see Lester's worried face, and I gave him the thumbs-up.

"Hey, Francis," I said as, to my amazement, the Ferret himself answered the phone. Three out of three: sometimes life is like that. "What's up? Shouldn't you be snoozing?"

"Very funny, Ms. Reece," he said testily. "For your information, I've been working on the job you gave me. Sean Patrick Macklin. Apparently all he has to do is spit on the sidewalk and he'll be back in jail. He has to report to his parole officer *daily*, if you please!"

"Oh yeah?" I said, elated.

"Yeah. And here's the kicker, sweets — he's disappeared."

"What?" I squeaked.

"Yup. Gone. Vanished. I listened in to the messages on Dr. Lowenstein's electronic mailbox and Macklin's parole officer is apoplectic. Seems your boy didn't call in last night and didn't report for work today. Not even his *mother* knows where he is." Francis tut-tutted happily. "Such a bad boy. It seems it's back to jail for little Sean."

I groaned. This didn't make much sense. Why would Macklin run now? Why not in a couple of months once he'd gotten everyone lulled into complacency? I couldn't figure it out. Maybe Wendy Murdoch was safe from him. And me? I guessed I'd just have to walk more softly and carry a bigger stick. And get that damned back door fixed.

"Thanks, Francis."

"*De rien,*" he cooed, showing off his French. "Do be careful, dearie. You're such a good customer."

To his credit, Lester didn't ask a single question as we drove back to town.

"I'll fill you in later," I told him as he deposited me in front of British Fish 'n Chips. "You deserve it. But not now, okay? I'm too tired and there's one more thing I have to do before I collapse."

"All right." A worried frown creased his sandy eyebrows. "You'll hate this," he said, "but will you be careful? Even though I was supposed to be in the kitchen drying my down vest, I heard what Callie said."

Just what I needed — another worrywart. "I'm just going to talk to a kid at a tea shop. What could happen to me there?"

Giving me a doubtful smile, he backed the Land Rover out of its parking space and drove off into the late afternoon gloom.

I felt more than a little gloomy myself as I pulled into my driveway and shut off the MG's motor. I was cold, my clothes and hair were sticky with salt, and I was ashamed of the way I had handled Tess. She should be in therapy, dammit, not sharpening her scalpel for an orchiectomy. And what had I done to help? I'd bullied her unmercifully, thinking she could take it. Surprise: she couldn't. I had caused that accident with the Zodiac. Because of me, Tess had almost drowned.

I hauled myself out of the car and into the house, turning on lights to brighten things up. Pansy and Repo were nowhere in sight, but Jeoffrey poked his head out from behind the armchair and waited to be summoned. Tired as I was, I positioned myself in the middle of the braided rug and called to him. He came confidently to me, tail in the air, twined once around my ankles, then stretched up, putting his front paws on my knees.

I scooped him into my arms, and for no reason I could name, I began to weep. Tears leaked from between my eyelids, and I dried them angrily on one sleeve.

"Mrrr? Mrrr?" he asked anxiously.

"It's nothing you can do anything about," I told him, sniffling. "Self-pity just has to run its course. Like a virus."

Putting him on the kitchen counter, I opened a can of food, divided it into three dishes, and called Repo. He appeared almost at once from the direction of my bedroom, looking decidedly guilty.

"What's up? Deserted your little buddy for an exotic female, have you?"

I lined up the dinner dishes and lifted Jeoffrey down to the dining spot, cocking an eyebrow at Repo. The cat was clearly in conflict. He eyed his dinner, looked longingly at the bedroom, then made up his mind to do neither. Instead he sat down with a *whuff*, hoisted a leg in the air, and began to wash his knee.

"Whatever," I said, hurrying into the bedroom,

shedding my sticky clothes as I went. Pansy gave me a proprietary look from a nest she had made between my pillows, stretched her toes luxuriously, and resumed her nap.

"Don't get too comfy," I told her. "This is just a foster home. You're Wendy's cat, not mine."

She opened one yellow eye, purred loudly, then covered her face with a paw.

I can't remember a shower ever feeling so good. I shampooed twice, rinsed with very hot water, toweled, brandished the hair dryer for a few moments, and was dressed in clean jeans and a fresh turtleneck in fifteen minutes flat. In the kitchen, I slapped two slices of cheese on bread with mayo, took a can of Pepsi to wash it down, grabbed my old leather jacket, and hurried back out to my car.

Julia was waiting for me at The Blethering Place, a pot of tea in front of her. Sandy, I noted, was seated two tables behind her. He looked solid and reassuring in his Harris tweed jacket, brown slacks, white shirt, and woolly vest. Replacing his teacup in its saucer, he patted his moustache with a napkin and nodded at me.

I took a chair across the table from Julia. "Thanks for coming." It suddenly occurred to me that so far in this case I had dealt with more than my share of lying ladies. That's the downside of my line of work — you get to see how people react under stress. Some come through with flying colors; some lie. I was thoroughly sick of all this, but I knew better than to take out my ire on Julia.

"I had to come," she said. "You're right. It's time to tell the whole truth." She looked up at me, clearly ashamed. "What I told you earlier, well, it *was* true. It just wasn't everything."

"Okay," I agreed, ordering coffee. "Tell me about your Christmas date."

Julia kept her eyes on the table. "Okay. Like I told you, we went out with these two basketball players. They'd been bugging us, calling us dykes because we didn't want to date them. So we agreed to go out with them once to get rid of them. We were supposed to go to a movie and for pizza and then come home. But we didn't. After the movie they drove to a sleazy bar in Esquimalt. The two of them drank a lot and kept pushing drinks on us. It was dark where we were sitting, and my date, Jesse, kept grabbing my . . . my breasts. He hurt me," she said looking up, her blue eyes filled with tears. "Finally Tess and I went to the bathroom and I told her I didn't want to go anywhere with these guys and that I was going to call a cab. But Tess had been drinking a little and she gets kind of aggressive when she's drunk. Well, she persuaded me that she'd handle them and everything would be all right. We went back to the table, she gave them a big speech, and they agreed to drive us home."

"But they didn't, did they?"

Julia shook her head. "No. They took us to a frat house just off campus. There was this awful party going on and the minute we walked in the door someone grabbed us — I mean literally grabbed us — took our coats and purses and started dancing with us, passing us around. Everyone was drunk, the music was so loud . . . I finally found Tess and we ran upstairs. I told her I was leaving, coat or no coat." She grimaced. "It had started to snow, but I figured I could get a cab. Anyone will take you to an Uplands address. But I couldn't get Tess to come with me. She'd met someone and she wanted to stay and talk, she said. I was furious. I told her she had two minutes to meet me on the front porch." She looked up at me again, eyes filled with tears. "But she didn't come. And I guess she got pretty drunk because the guy who took her there, Brian Conway, raped her in the pantry just off the kitchen. She called me up at four in the morning, in hysterics, and told me pretty much what happened. And she made me promise not to tell."

I didn't understand. "Why not, Julia?"

"Because Conway . . . threatened her," she whispered. "He scared the hell out of her. And he hurt her really bad. He bragged that she wasn't the first girl he'd raped and she wouldn't be the last."

I felt sick, but I needed to press for facts. "Did she see a doctor?"

"No. She was too ashamed."

I ground my teeth. How many Tesses were there on campuses all over North America? Thousands, I bet.

"So tell me what happened next."

"Well, what I told you earlier. That part of it was true, anyway. I called and called her, but she just wouldn't talk to me. She changed her class schedule, found new friends." Her tears dripped onto the tablecloth. "You know, I think she blames me. I think she feels that if I'd waited for her, the rape wouldn't have happened. Maybe I should have waited. But I was angry at her for wanting to stay and I was afraid. So I left. I ran out on her."

"I don't know if that's what she feels," I told Julia. "I do know she's filled with rage and about to do something that will land her in prison. Unless . . ." I paused dramatically, deliberately.

"Unless what?"

"Unless we get the police to pick up her rapist before Tess and her friends get to him. That will short-circuit their plans."

"It would, wouldn't it?" she said hopefully.

I didn't want to give her time to think about this. "Where can the police find him, Julia?"

She paused, then came to a decision. "On campus. In the dorm. Thompson House. He rooms with the guy I went out with, Jesse McGregor."

I squeezed her hand reassuringly. "Will you tell this to the police? Go with them to make the identification?"

"This is going to be awful, isn't it?" she asked, her lower lip trembling. "I'll have to go to court, too. And everybody will talk about it. About me. About Tess. Like it was our fault those guys acted the way they did."

"I won't lie to you. It's not going to be a picnic. But you can't let this jerk walk around free any longer. He needs to be put away before he hurts other women." If he hadn't already done so, I thought.

She chewed her lip. "All right," she said in a small voice.

I squeezed her hand again. "Atta girl."

"How do I . . . do it?" she wanted to know. "Do I just walk into the police station or what?"

"Look behind you." I pointed to Sandy sitting

innocently reading the paper and eating a muffin. "That's Detective Alexander. A friend of mine. If you like, we can go over and talk to him right now."

"Will you come with me?" she asked anxiously.

"Sure. I'll make introductions and then leave you two alone. Will that be okay?"

She nodded.

"Atta girl." I got up and held her chair.

As I turned into the driveway beside my house, preoccupied with thoughts of Tess's ordeal, I suddenly realized a car had pulled in behind me. Macklin? Unlikely. Still, I cut my motor and lights and reached for my .357, remembering too late that I hadn't taken it with me today. It was still in its shoebox. So I climbed out of the MG and stood in the driveway, hands on my hips. If he wanted me, let him come for me.

The car behind mine doused its lights and I blinked a few times, trying to restore my night vision. Cratered and huge, the full moon sailed out from behind a ragged cloud, leaving me no place to hide.

"Caitlin," a low voice called out the driver's window.

Then I remembered. Diana. Oh brother. If there ever was a bad time, this was it. As I walked down the driveway toward her car, she got out to meet me.

"I've been lied to by everyone in this case," I said belligerently. "Everyone. It's like the bloody flu — everyone's got it. So look me in the eye and tell me one thing, just one thing. Tell me you aren't Artemis."

She blinked a few times and in the pitiless silver light of the pocked moon, I saw her hesitate. My stomach clenched and I realized with a sinking feeling that I had really wanted her to be innocent, to be completely ignorant of the madness that had claimed Gillian and Tess.

"I've certainly heard of the group," she said. "And I knew Gillian and a few of my other students were involved. I knew, too, that they hoped for my . . . participation. But I refused. No, I wasn't Artemis."

The rush of relief I felt was dizzying.

"Do you believe me?" she asked.

"Believe you?" I asked. I was too tired to try to figure the angles, to try to figure why she'd lie to me. I know now I should've tried harder. Because I didn't believe her. Not completely, anyhow. But I needed to believe her, and so I lied. "Yeah, I believe you." I said what I wished were true. Because I couldn't go to bed with the woman who was Artemis. And I had a pretty good idea that bed was where we were going. So I didn't grill her; I didn't push.

"I'm glad," she said.

"Me too. Come on in." I climbed the front steps, unlocked the door, and stepped back to let her enter. She took off her coat and hung it on the coat tree as I locked the door behind us and reached for the lights.

"No," she said, her hand closing over mine, gripping it tightly. "No lights yet." She stepped closer, then, both hands in my hair, drew my head down and kissed me. This was no tender, gentle, exploratory kiss, either: this was a real tooth-chipper.

Her desire found an unexpected echo in me and, as we devoured each other, I thought I might suffocate from the sheer, knee-weakening passion of it.

"You have no idea how much I've wanted this," she told me shakily, stepping back a little, a disembodied voice in the darkness of the hall. "From the first time I saw you, this is what I've had on my mind. This is all I could think about. I'm sorry."

I pulled her close. "You hardly need to apologize," I said, against her lips. "And it's been on my mind, too."

She made a soft sound that might have been a sigh. "No more talk now," she said, opening her lips under mine. I needed no encouragement and as my questing tongue sought hers, I felt her shiver. Our kiss deepened and Diana moved against me with an eloquent urgency.

I broke off our kiss and took her hands in mine. "Come on," I said, the two of us navigating an unsteady course to my bedroom.

The full moon had turned my bedroom ebony and silver, *chiaroscuro,* magical, a dreamscape. I raised Diana's hand to my lips and kissed her palm. Her back was to the window, her features totally in shadow, the moon a brilliant silver disc behind her, and for just a moment, I knew that all the assurances she had given me were lies. For a moment I fancied her the mythical Artemis, cruel huntress, harrier of men, but then a cloud sniffed out the moon and she was just Diana again — a woman who wanted me. And who I wanted.

I put my hands on her hips and drew her to me. She came eagerly, and we kissed again, my body feeling scalded where she pressed against me.

"God," she said, kissing my cheek, my throat. "I can't . . . forgive me." I was about to ask her what for when she pulled my turtleneck out of my jeans and ran her hands over my ribs, finally stopping at my breasts.

"Oh," she exclaimed, in a choked voice. "I'd almost forgotten how good this feels."

Then she took my hand and placed it on her own breast. "Please," she whispered.

I understood. Putting my hands under her sweater, I tugged it over her head. Her hands on my shoulders, she stood with her eyes closed, head back, lips parted. I bent to kiss a line from her collarbone to one breast and as my lips closed over her small nipple, she shuddered violently.

Sliding my hands down her bare back, I knelt and peeled her wool slacks off, kissing the soft warm skin of her stomach as I did so. She kicked the slacks aside and I felt her hands fasten in my hair as I moved my lips down her stomach to her thighs. I took her small, silken buttocks in my hands and kissed the mossy mat of her pubic hair. She pulled my head hard against her, exclaiming aloud in pleasure and I caressed her thighs, my fingers finding the wet warmth between them.

I started to shrug out of my jacket, but she stopped me.

"Don't take it off," she whispered. "Come here."

"All right," I agreed, understanding what she wanted.

Straightening up, I clasped her to me, sliding one knee between her legs.

"Yes," she whispered, snaking her arms around me and grabbing two handfuls of my jacket. She

183

leaned her head back and I kissed her throat, her jaw, her ear. When she moved her head to offer me her mouth, I was not gentle. Gentleness was not what she wanted.

She moaned, drawing me closer, and I put one hand between her legs, cupping the soft, springy hair. My fingers found the hard bud of her clitoris, then the wet warmth at her center, and as I slipped first one finger then two inside her, she gasped and moved violently against me. She didn't give me a chance to find her rhythm. Instead, she reached for my hand, held it still, and began a rhythm of her own against it, making her own pleasure. It seemed as though she had hardly begun when she arched against me, cried out, and then was still, shuddering and gasping. Finally she took a deep breath.

"Thank you," she said.

"You don't need to thank me," I told her, bending to lift her onto the bed.

She ran her hands over the worn leather of my bomber jacket. "Is this your armor?"

"Maybe," I said. "It was my dad's flight jacket. He was an air force pilot."

She slid between the sheets, pulling the comforter up to her chin. "I might be wrong about you," she said. "I thought you were an alchemist, but you might still be a warrior."

I stepped out of my sneakers, tossed my jacket over a chair, followed it with my turtleneck and jeans, and gently slid in beside her. "I'm just me, Diana," I told her. "I can't name the shadow or anything else. I'm just . . . someone who tries."

She turned to embrace me and the shock of her

naked flesh meeting mine was electric, visceral. I groaned and pulled her close. We lay like that for a few moments and then a strange thing happened. I felt Diana's poise, her wry humor, desert her. I felt her shiver. I felt her break — a subtle movement in her shoulders, a letting go. And I knew that whatever she might say to me in the next few moments would be absolutely the truth.

"Caitlin," she whispered as though she had never said my name before, "you must promise not to hate me."

"For what?" I asked, mouth dry.

"For the future. For my requiring you to be merciful."

I didn't understand, but I held her close anyway and stroked her hair and kissed her forehead.

"Do you promise?" she insisted.

"I promise," I said, not because I understood, but because it was so terribly important to her. "I promise." And then, as I lay quietly holding her, my terrible fatigue overcame me. "I'm sorry," I said, kissing her eyelids. "I'm beat. I need to sleep for awhile."

Diana touched my face and said softly, "Later, then." And after a moment, "Goodnight."

That seemed fine to me, so I burrowed down into the mattress. But then a strange thing happened. At least I think a strange thing happened, because I was more than halfway unconscious. I thought Diana got out of bed, went somewhere and came back. I thought she bent over me and kissed me softly on the cheek. I thought she said, "I'm the one who is sorry," and after a moment, "Goodbye." But I must have been wrong because my last memory was of holding Diana's body to mine as I slid down the dark tunnel of sleep.

When the phone rang, I fell out of bed reaching for it. Disoriented, nine-tenths asleep, I yanked it off the night table and yelled into the receiver. "What?"

"Caitlin, it's Callie," a hysterical voice called. "They're going to do it!"

"Do what?" I demanded, scooting around on the floor, finally getting my feet under me. Snapping on the table lamp, I stood up, noting with a pang of loss that I was alone.

"What we talked about," she wailed. "They're going to cut some guy's balls off. Gillian and Ruth grabbed him. They had him stashed somewhere for a day or so, but now they've got him in the basement. They're getting him ready."

"What?" I said. "The Oak Bay Police must have grabbed Tess's rapist by now. Gillian's made a mistake."

"I know he isn't the one," Callie wailed. "Tess said so. Oh, it doesn't make any sense! Gillian and the others had planned all along to make an example of Tess's rapist, but for some reason they changed their minds. Yesterday they picked up someone else."

"Dammit," I said. I hadn't counted on this. I figured that when the Daughters couldn't find Tess's rapist, they'd retrench. Think things over. I thought it was important to them that the vengeance be personal — an eye for an eye. I never dreamed they would abandon their plans and just select someone else. It didn't make any sense.

"Caitlin, you've got to stop them. Please. I don't want to see Gillian go to prison."

"Callie, where are you?"

"At the Land's End Deli-Mart. In a phone booth."

"Stay put. I'm on my way."

I threw my clothes on and as I was jamming my feet into my sneakers, I called Sandy. Just to be sure Callie wasn't mistaken.

"It's Caitlin," I said when his sleepy voice answered. "Just say yes or no. Did you pick Brian Conway up earlier tonight?"

"Yes. Just after we talked."

"Do you think you can make him for the Full Moon Rapist?"

He hesitated.

"C'mon Sandy. I need to know."

"Chances are he's the one. Our evidence indicates it — evidence we never released to the press. But you know as well as I do that whether he goes down for this depends on the CP's office. We'll certainly do our part. Oh, and you didn't hear any of this from me."

"Thanks. Sorry for waking you."

I ground my teeth. Those melodramatic fools up at Land's End were probably about to kill someone. For nothing. If Sandy was right — and I had a gut feeling he was — the cause of the Daughters' ire was even now answering questions in an interview room. It really was all over. Someone needed to communicate this to the Land's End ladies and I guessed I got the job of message-bearer. Great. I hustled into the closet for my .357, thrust my hand into the shoebox, and felt . . . nothing. Dumbfounded, I grabbed the shoebox and shook it, but it was clearly empty. What the hell? Hadn't I put my gun away after that awful scene with Diana the other night. Shit. I just couldn't remember. Heaving the shoebox back into the closet, I ran for my dresser. There, in the drawer under my sweaters, I found my short-barreled .38, my backup gun. I broke the action, made certain the weapon was loaded, and with a curse, shoved it into the waistband of my jeans. With a grab for my bomber jacket, I raced out the door to my car.

It was when I was putting the key in the ignition that it hit me again — Diana had not been in bed beside me when I awoke. Sometime in the night, she had gone. Home, I guessed. I felt another stab of loss, then shook my head. There'd be time enough for Diana after this was over.

"What are you going to do?" Callie asked fearfully as we parked on the road just down from Crowley's estate.

"I don't know," I told her. "I'll think of something."

"Here's a key to the basement door," she said. "It leads into the old coal cellar. It's empty now. The room . . . the place where they have him is at the end of the hall. I'll wait here for you," she said, shrinking down inside her parka. "Please try to talk them out of it. Or . . . stop them."

I thought of the .38 in my jeans. Oh, I intended to talk them out of it all right.

The key fit smoothly into the basement door lock, and the cylinder turned soundlessly. I twisted the knob and eased the door open. It swung without a murmur of complaint. Obviously the girls used this door a lot. Inside, I smelled mustiness and a faintly acidic tang that I couldn't identify. Switching on my penlight, I shone it around. Just as Callie had explained, this was indeed the coal cellar. In the outside wall was a boarded-up chute and a window above it. The rest of the room was absolutely empty, save for coal dust. I refused to even think about sneezing.

Inching open the hall door, I put my penlight into my pocket, took off my gloves and flexed my fingers a little, then unzipped my jacket and drew the .38. With a mental apology to Brendan, my firearms instructor, who believed that guns ought to be defensive weapons, I flattened myself against the wall and crept down the hall toward the room at the end. As things turned out, I needn't have worried about concealing myself. Entire football teams could have scrimmaged in the cellar and not shaken these ladies' concentration.

I peeked around the corner of the makeshift operating room and there they were, gathered around the table like a coven of witches. Gillian and Ruth, in black pants and turtlenecks, their white armbands proudly proclaiming them to be Daughters of Artemis, stood at the end of the table, arms crossed, looking on in evident fascination. Another woman — a small blonde I recognized from earlier today — stood with Tess on one side of the table. And on the table, stark naked, bound spread-eagled, lay Sean Macklin. A drugged and insensible Sean Macklin.

I was too pumped up to try to understand this. Taking three strides into the room, I assumed a shooter's stance.

"Back off from the table," I told them.

Gillian and Ruth saw me first and the astonishment in their eyes was almost comical.

"Against the wall!" I snarled. "Move!"

Gillian and Ruth backed away until they stood against the far wall. "So what are you going to do, shoot us?" Gillian laughed. "C'mon, Miss Tough Guy. You ought to shoot this Sean Macklin piece of shit here. Why don't you?"

"Caitlin," Ruth said silkily, "just listen to us for a minute." An intense-looking woman with long, dark, Medusa-like hair, she fixed me with an unblinking stare. "This man is a convicted rapist, out of jail on some wrong-headed work release program. We've heard that he threatened your life. Why do you care about him, anyhow? Let us take care of him, see that he gets what he deserves."

What was going on here? How in hell did they know anything about Sean Macklin, let alone about me? I felt as though I'd stumbled onto a movie set where everyone but me knew their lines. Maybe I was dreaming. Maybe I'd wake up in a moment and find myself in bed, Repo at my feet.

"C'mon, Caitlin, just turn and walk away," Ruth urged. "It'll be easy."

The crazy thing was, it *would* be easy, and for an instant I was tempted. But just for an instant.

"I can't," I told Ruth.

"Maybe not this time," she said, "but it's written all over your face that you'd like to. Another time you will walk away, because whether you know it or not, you're one of the Daughters of Artemis."

I laughed, but even to me it sounded hollow. There was a certain amount of truth in what she had said. Angry with myself, I put a sneer in my voice. "No, I'm not one of you."

"Take the scalpel, Tess," the blonde at the table said, bringing me back to the business at hand.

As I looked back to Macklin's groin, I realized, nope, this was definitely no dream. He had been shaved and painted with Betadine scrub, the iodine in the liquid giving his skin a ghoulish orange cast. His penis, a limp pink slug, was clipped back out of the way and I realized that in a couple of minutes he was going to be minus his balls.

Tess took the scalpel.

"Put the scalpel down, Tess," I ordered, turning my gun on her.

"Oh, come off it. You won't shoot her," Gillian said confidently. "Hell, you were hired to find her and bring her home. You even saved her life. How will you explain to her sister that you *shot* her? Go ahead, Tess."

For a split second, I was tempted to walk up to

Tess and try to take the scalpel away. But I was certain that all of us would only end up in a wrestling match. A wrestling match which I would probably lose. Shit. There was no good solution to this.

"Now make a cut in the scrotum like I showed you," I heard Ellie tell Tess. "Right there, right there where I've drawn a line with magic marker."

"Yeah, go ahead, Tess," I said. "Let yourself be used. Brian Conway, Sean Macklin, what's the difference?"

She gave me a quick look, full of doubts she couldn't quite hide. Good. Perhaps in Tess's mind there *was* a difference. I needed to capitalize on that.

"I hope you've noticed that none of the other Daughters is risking five to fifteen in Parksville," I continued. "Nope, they're saving that little treat for you. They don't care about helping you take revenge on Conway. In fact, they probably don't care that the Full Moon Rapist has been caught."

"Like hell he has!" Gillian said. "We'd have heard about it."

"No one's heard about it. The police just picked him up," I told her with a mental apology to Sandy. "So there's no need for any of this."

"She's lying," Gillian told Tess confidently. "Just get on with it."

"But what if I'm not?" I asked Tess. "What then?"

Tess clutched the scalpel tightly in one hand, but she did turn to look at me. I had the faintest glimmering of an idea in my mind, but it demanded that I keep her talking and get a little closer to her. I took a slow step forward.

"I'm telling you the truth," I said. "The Oak Bay Police picked up the Full Moon Rapist tonight. And guess who he is? Brian Conway."

She looked stricken. "How did . . . who . . .?"

"Julia talked. I put two and two together."

She blinked a few times. "It's too late for all that," she said. "For the law's kind of justice. One rapist will serve our purpose as well as another. And when we're through with this one, he'll never rape anyone again."

"Don't kid yourself," I said, shuffling closer. "This guy may not be able to get it up to actually do it *himself,* but there are plenty of proxies in the world."

"What do you mean?" she asked, genuinely puzzled.

"Think, Tess. What is rape, anyhow? It has almost nothing to do with sex apart from the object the man uses to batter the woman with. Take that away and he'll find another. Haven't you thought that through?" I waved my gun at Macklin. "This guy has been a woman-hater most of his life. Nothing is going to change that. When he comes around and finds himself castrated, he'll be wild. Completely out of control. If I were a betting person, I'd bet his next crime will be one hell of a grisly murder. A murder you'll have driven him to. And think of what fools you'll look . . . all this drama for nothing. Tess, the Full Moon Rapist's been *caught.*"

Tess began to sob. I edged still closer.

"Tess," Ellie demanded in a flat voice. "Don't listen to her. She probably *is* lying."

I took one more slow step forward, transferred my weight to my left foot, and was just about to draw my right foot back for a good kick at Tess's scalpel hand, when a voice called from behind me.

"Caitlin . . . stop. And don't turn around. I have a gun."

It was Diana. And suddenly, all the pieces meshed. Her interest in me in the first place, the crazy late-night visit that resulted in my babbling my head off about Macklin, the torrid scene in my bedroom a few hours ago . . . I felt like a complete fool. She'd used me. And worse than that, I'd invited it. An icy anger washed over me, and suddenly I didn't care what Diana did. I knew whose gun Diana had all right — mine — but I had to do what I had to do.

"So shoot me," I said, bracing myself and delivering my best point-after kick to Tess's right hand. The scalpel flew from her grasp and to my satisfaction, slid under a cabinet. I spun around, intending to rush Diana, but she was quicker than I thought. And more cold-blooded. She had the barrel of my .357 pointed straight at my head, hammer cocked. "Diana," I croaked, intending to tell her to put the gun down and to be bloody careful doing it — I'd fixed the .357 so a feather would set it off after the hammer was cocked — but I might as well have saved my breath. With a horrifying sense of disbelief, I saw her finger close over the trigger. I threw myself to my right — the gun pulls to the shooter's right — but there simply wasn't time to get out of the way. I saw the muzzle flash orange, heard the big gun's *boom,* and felt what seemed to be a cannon ball hit me just above my left ear. A mushroom cloud of pain erupted in my head and I was suddenly deaf, blind, and boneless, helplessly plunging over a cliff in the middle of the night, tumbling into an icy black sea.

CHAPTER TEN

I was a handful of brittle leaves, carried on a cold, black wind. I was a clatter of mouse's bones, scrabbled from some nameless grave; I was a pair of ragged claws, scuttling across the bottom of the sea. And then . . . I was floating under a gibbous moon with the sea beneath me calling my name.

"Caitlin," it murmured, the sound a thousand miles away. This seemed familiar; I had been here before. A sense of urgency flooded me. I needed to do something, respond in some way. But what? How? I decided to sink back into the blackness.

"Caitlin," the voice insisted, and I felt my body being shaken. And with the knowledge that I had a body came, reluctantly, consciousness, and with consciousness, pain.

"Lee me lo," I moaned.

"God, I'm so glad you're all right," a woman's voice said. But why was she whispering? I turned my head. My right ear worked fine, but there was definitely something wrong with the left one.

"All right" was definitely debatable. "Ha," I said, trying to sit up. "Jesus," I grunted, holding my head in my hands. The pain was Olympic-caliber. Top notch. Aspirins wouldn't touch this. And when my fingers found the mass of clotted blood in my hair just above my ear, I knew I was in big trouble. Then I remembered. I'd been shot. That explained my left-side hearing loss. God, maybe I really *was* deaf. But was I blind, too? Why was everything so dark?

"Who's there?" I whispered. "Where am I?"

"It's Callie," a voice quavered. "You're in the coal cellar. Gillian put you here. I was waiting outside like you told me when I heard the shot. So I came to see what had happened. Can you walk if I help you? We could make it to your car."

"Wait," I said. "What are they doing — Diana and the others?"

"Arguing," Callie told me. "Gillian and Ruth still want to castrate that man. But now Tess won't go through with it. Neither will Ellie. They're afraid Diana might have killed you. And Tess is afraid you were telling the truth about the Full Moon Rapist."

"And what about Diana?" I asked evenly. "Isn't she afraid?"

"I don't think so," Callie said. "She came in to check on you once and told us you'd be all right. No, she's . . . she's just sitting in the corner listening to them argue."

"Where's the gun I had?" I asked her.

"I've got it. I picked it up when no one was looking. They think of me as part of the furniture," she said bitterly. "No one notices what I do."

"Help me stand up," I told her. "Put the gun in my hand." She did, and I stuck the .38 in the waistband of my jeans. "Now you have a choice. You can come along and help me or you can disappear. But if you come along, everyone will know which side you're on. Including Gillian."

"I'll come and help. Gillian didn't even check to see if you were alive when she dragged you in here," she said indignantly. "She's worse than Diana."

I thought about Diana holding my own Smith and Wesson on me, cocking it, then slowly pulling the trigger. "Maybe. Maybe not. In any event, they deserve each other."

"Why are you doing this for them?" she asked. "Why not just call the police and turn them all in?"

"Don't think that the notion hasn't occurred to me. But if I do that, a couple of innocent people will be hurt, too."

"Oh yeah? Like who?"

"Tess for one. And you for another."

She thought about this for a moment. "But we're guilty, too. Maybe not as guilty as Gillian and Diana, but we're still guilty."

"I know," I said wearily. "But that's between you and your consciences. I have to do things my way, Callie. If they haven't hurt Macklin and if he's still out so he can't identify anyone, I'll give them the chance to walk away from this."

"They don't deserve it," she said stubbornly. "But tell me what I have to do."

We took them by surprise. When Callie and I walked into the makeshift operating room Diana was indeed sitting in the corner. She watched, or listened to, the others arguing. And arguing they were. Gillian and Ruth stood on one side of the table, Tess and Ellie on the other, Macklin stretched out like a piece of pale meat between them.

"Nobody moves!" I yelled, letting some of the fury I felt infuse my voice. "Not one bloody inch! The mood I'm in, I'll blow any of you straight to hell." Four pairs of eyes goggled at me as though I had just arisen from the dead. Well, maybe I had.

"Toss that gun over here," I told Diana, taking aim at her. "No tricks and no sudden moves. Use one finger."

She gave me an inscrutable look, then reached slowly down beside her and brought the .357 up, holding it by the trigger guard.

"Over here," I said. "Just throw it nice and easy."

To my surprise, she did so. It landed with a satisfying *thunk* just in front of my feet.

"Pick it up," I told Callie. "And stay out of my line of fire."

She did so and handed me the gun. I took it and stuck it in my pocket.

"Well, shit," Gillian said, looking from me to Callie. "So we finally find out what side you're on."

"Yeah," Callie said staunchly. "You finally find out."

"Shut up," I told Gillian. "The last thing we need here is anyone's smart mouth." I looked from one to the other of them. "Listen up. I should turn all of you in. After all, you're guilty of attempted murder."

"But *he's* guilty of —" Ellie said.

"You shut up, too," I told her cruelly. "I'm talking about me, not him. Your mentor here, the brave Artemis, nearly blew my head off. And you four are accessories to a capital crime. One that I can make stick. So shut up and listen. It's very simple. You have a choice. You can get the hell out of here now or you can talk to the cops when they get here in about half an hour. You decide."

Gillian swallowed and looked across the table at Diana. I understood what was going on and I decided to subtract Diana from the equation for now. "She stays," I told Gillian. "She's not part of the deal. I have a score to settle with her."

"*Gillian!*" Ruth said urgently. "Come on. She's giving us a chance. Let's get out of here."

"Can we really go?" Tess asked me, looking sidelong at Gillian.

"Yeah, beat it," I told her. "Go to Julia's place."

She opened her mouth to protest, and I yelled her down. "*No arguments!* Just do it. And call me tomorrow because you can be damned sure I want to talk to you."

With a final look at Gillian, Tess and Ellie sidled past me and out the door.

"So?" I asked Gillian. "What's it gonna be?"

Gillian looked again at Diana, and to my surprise, Diana answered her.

"The lady's being merciful," Diana told her. "It's a good deal. Take it."

"But —"

Diana held up a hand. "There'll be another day for you and Ruth. Another chance to prove yourselves. Go on," she told them kindly.

"What about you?" Gillian wanted to know.

Diana shrugged. "That's up to Caitlin. She's quite within her rights doing anything she chooses." She gave me a long, slow look. "My fate is in her hands, and I trust her to make the best decision."

That's when I finally accepted the fact that Diana was crazy. Certifiably nuts. She thought this was another arcane drama we were acting out. Another play. A tragedy with great-sounding poetic lines in Greek and Latin and noble roles for both of us. Her fate in my hands indeed.

"Do as she says and get out of here," I told Gillian. "And before you do, cut this guy loose and get his clothes."

Ruth unfastened the knots holding Macklin's arms and legs and gathered up a bundle of clothes that had been tossed in the corner.

"Callie, help Ruth dress him," I said.

Glaring at me, the bloodthirsty Gillian slumped against the wall, pouting. She was having no part of this forced retreat.

"Did he see any of you?" I asked Ruth.

"I don't think so. We put a pillowcase over his head when we grabbed him. He may have heard us, but I'm pretty sure he didn't see anything."

"What did you give him and how long has he been out?"

"A veterinary tranquilizer. Acepromaxine. He's

had two shots and he's been out for about three hours. He'll be out for another half an hour."

"Okay. You and Gillian load him into your car and take him home."

Ruth frowned. "Home? Where's that?"

"Look in the phone book under Macklin. It's an address in Saanich. Dump him on the front doorstep, ring the buzzer, and drive like hell." I snorted. "Just wait till he tries to explain to his parole officer what happened."

"Gillian?" Ruth asked.

Gillian seemed to shake herself. She looked once at me, once at Diana, then focused on Macklin. "All right. But this isn't the end," she warned me. "You'll hear from us."

"Oh, I'm sure I will," I said. "You'll find another wrong to avenge."

"Rape needs to be avenged," she told me, white around the lips.

"Maybe it does and maybe it doesn't, Gillian. But you don't have the right to make that decision." I felt like an ass delivering this lecture, but I made myself continue. "Listen to me. The Full Moon Rapist is off the streets for good." I crossed my fingers on that one. "This guy has been turned loose by the system, and I don't like it any more than you do. But both men are now none of your concern."

"Don't think we can't find others," she asserted. "There are plenty of rapists we can use to get our message across."

"I know," I said, not unkindly. "I know. Just get this one on his feet and out of here."

Between them, Ruth and Gillian pushed the limp Macklin into a sitting position, then, supporting him, dragged him from the room. "Give them a hand with doors, will you?" I asked Callie. She trailed along after them, clearly reluctant to go.

That left me alone with Diana.

"You didn't call the police, did you?" she asked me, smiling a cat's smile, full of secrets.

"No."

"I thought not." She looked me up and down. "Now what?"

"I don't know," I told her, leaning on the edge of the table that Macklin had only recently occupied. "I'm tired, I feel like hell, and my head hurts. I guess, though, I want to understand why."

"Ah, that," she said. "Always asking the hard questions, aren't you?"

"Just answer, please. Can you?"

She regarded me levelly. "What are you having so much trouble understanding?"

I shrugged. "All of this. Why you . . . used me. Why you agreed to be a part of this."

She smiled again. "Because it was all so . . . right. Don't you see that?"

"No," I said, but that was not completely the truth. Part of me *did* see the rightness of it and understood Diana's screwy logic. The part of me that was very much like Diana resonated to her like a plucked string. She knew it and I knew it.

"Say what you like, I know you see it," she told me with her uncanny perception. "But answer the question I asked you first. Now what?"

"You mean what am I going to do with you?"

"Yes. That."

I came to an abrupt decision. "Nothing. You can go."

She laughed. "What? You're not going to turn me in? Cuff me? Drag me screaming to the arms of the law?"

"No, I'm not."

"I suppose I ought to ask why not."

I shrugged. "Ask if you like." It was a good question. Why wasn't I turning her in? Well, it was complicated. It was *my* life she tried to take, *my* blood she spilled and if there was to be a reckoning, I wanted to be the one to mete it out. In that respect, Diana and I were appallingly alike. But I had already decided that punishment would be inappropriate. "You don't need punishment. You need help. Please get it, Diana. Get someone who can help you salvage yourself. That's why I'm not turning you in. The system would only destroy you. Warehouse you somewhere. I'm giving you a chance. Take it."

"How merciful you are," she said sarcastically.

I hadn't expected that. Stung, I countered in like fashion. "Yeah, aren't I though. So just beat it."

"What does one have to do to make you really angry?" she asked. "Angry enough to kill? You *would* kill, wouldn't you, if you were pushed far enough?"

"No more, Diana," I said, closing my eyes. "Just go."

When I opened my eyes, she was gone. I sat there for a moment, too tired to move. Was this what Diana had meant when she had asked me not to hate her for requiring me to be merciful? I

204

guessed so. I guessed she had had this planned all along and had counted on the fact that I wouldn't turn her in. Mercy. I snorted. *Had* I been merciful, letting her go? Had I given her what she wanted? I shook my head. Only Diana could answer that.

CHAPTER ELEVEN
Saturday

"So, what's the verdict?" I asked Gray Ng. "Does it need suturing or can you fix it?"

I was sitting on the edge of Gray's bathtub, and she was busy snipping my hair away, pulling the clots of blood loose, and working at the whole mess with warm water and cotton balls. "Ah," she said finally, her dark eyes narrowed in concentration.

"Ah, what?"

"Ah, I can finally see the wound."

"Great," I told her, my stomach clenching.

"Yes, I believe I can repair it. It's not deep, and the edges of the wound really can't be sutured. It's fortunately just a graze. I can clean it but you will have to be careful to take care of it. Otherwise it will become infected. About your hearing loss, though, I can do nothing. You must see a specialist."

"Okay," I sighed. "Clean away."

As Gray continued to snip and dab, I began to tell her the whole sorry tale, mostly to take my mind off the pain. Once started though, I found I couldn't stop. Eventually, I ran out of steam and fell silent.

"Things may not have turned out as you wished," Gray said, "but they concluded satisfactorily nonetheless. Your depression seems unwarranted."

"Maybe you're right," I told her. "The Daughters of Artemis are temporarily disbanded, Tess has been separated from her new friends, Callie's job has been saved, Macklin's balls are intact, although he'll soon be back in prison for violating his parole, and hey, Sandy has the Full Moon Rapist behind bars. We hope. So I guess I ought to be whooping it up. Why do I feel so glum, then?"

"Only you know why."

"Yeah, I know why. It's Diana."

"Perhaps you ought not to feel so badly for her," Gray said, pasting a final strip of tape to my head. "You gave her another chance, after all. Few people would have done that."

"Yeah," I sighed, standing up to examine the very professional-looking bandage she had made. "Where did you learn to do this?" I asked.

She was silent for so long I decided that I must

207

have offended her by prying into her past. It was an unspoken agreement between us that I never quizzed Gray about her life in Vietnam. Clod, I reproached myself.

"Cu Chi," she said finally.

"Oh," I answered, thinking furiously. Jesus. This was the first thing Gray had ever told me about herself and I had absolutely no idea what she was talking about. Cu Chi. I made a mental note to stop by the library as soon as I had time.

She must have sensed my confusion because she smiled and put a hand on my shoulder. "Come. I will make coffee," she said. "The sun will rise in a few minutes. We can sit on the deck and watch the dawn."

A hand under my elbow, Gray led me to a little sunroom at the back of the house. "Sit here." She offered me what was clearly her chair.

"Hey, I can sit over there," I protested.

"Nonsense," she said. "Then you will not be able to see the sun as it rises over Mount Baker. It is quite splendid this time of year." She pushed me gently down into the chair and, to my extreme embarrassment, this tiny woman drew up a footstool for me to put my feet on. "You need to rest," she said. "I am going to make coffee now." As she left the room, she called to me. "There is a book of poetry on the table beside you. I marked one poem for you to read."

I sighed and picked up the book. It was poems by Marge Piercy, *The Moon Is Always Female*. I am not fond of contemporary poetry, but I thought, okay. Anything to humor Gray. The book fell open at a poem called "For Strong Women" and I began to read. The poem opened with the extraordinary image of a woman standing on tiptoe, hefting a barbell, and trying to sing Boris Godunov. I laughed, as the author had intended me to, and then skimmed to a passage Gray had underlined. A chorus of voices demanded, with questions like hammer blows, why I wasn't feminine, soft, quiet, dead. I could have named every one of the voices that spoke in my head — father, uncle, brother, colleague.

"Jesus," I muttered. "Who is this writer and why have I never heard of her?"

Hearing Gray come up behind me, I put the book down.

"No," she said, placing a mug of coffee on the table beside me, and perching on the footstool. "Continue. Please read aloud."

I cleared my throat and began, but after a stanza I broke off. It hurt too much. "No. I can't."

"Why can't you?" she asked. "Because you fear those lines might be true?"

"I . . . I don't like to read aloud," I lied. Gray was right. I did fear that the lines might be true. And it was a truth I didn't want to deal with right now. I blinked away the tears that had started to fill my eyes.

"That poem was written for you," she said quietly.

"No!" I cried. "I'm not strong. People want me to be, people think I am, but really I'm not. I'm just like everyone else. I do the best I can. But sometimes I feel weak and frightened too."

"You are never weak, and though you may be

frightened, fear never prevents you from doing what you believe to be right," Gray said.

"I never wanted to be strong," I whispered. "I can't carry people on my shoulders. I can only do what I'm able to. And it's never enough, Gray. Whatever I do is never enough."

She smiled the thousand-year-old smile that always made me feel that inside that small body there was someone other than the Vietnamese refugee she professed to be. "You must let your friends help you, then," she said. "Didn't the poet say that we will all be afraid until we are all strong together? Because we are all afraid, Caitlin. Don't you know that? Every one of us. Afraid. But we must carry on. And those of us who are a little less afraid, a little stronger, must help the others."

I sniffled a little and wiped my eyes on my sleeve. "All right," I conceded. "But you're wrong about one thing, though."

"Oh?"

"Yeah. The damned poem wasn't written for me. It was written for someone special. Someone who has . . . a tiger's heart. Not me."

"It was written for whoever it speaks to." She pointed to the window. "Look."

I looked. In a steel-blue sky, behind the jagged white tooth at the top of Mount Baker, the sun rose in a riot of flame and peach. Another cold sunrise. A winter sunrise. Dammit, it was March. Where was spring?

"Another day," Gray said. "Another chance." And before I could reply, she asked, "Have you finished your coffee?"

"Well, yes."

"Good," she said, rising to her feet. "Go home and sleep. I have work to do. Today the bay horse will talk to me about posts."

I didn't doubt it for a minute. Gathering up my things, I went.

CHAPTER TWELVE

There was a note tacked to my front door. Unfolding it, I read:

Caitlin, I dropped by to ask you to take care of Pansy for a while. I'm going to look for a job up-island. Thanks.

Wendy

"Phooey," I yelled, and scrunched the note into a ball, firing it into the side yard. I unlocked the door and stormed into the house, heaving my jacket over the couch. Too tired to make an extra trip to the bedroom, I decided to stuff the .38 and the .357 under my jacket for the time being. And because I felt like making a nest, I pulled down the blinds and closed the curtains. Darkness. Give me darkness.

I called Sandy, Tess, and Perry just to touch bases briefly, then the locksmith and the glazier, and finally Tonia, to beg off on the trip to Vancouver. She said she would come over later with Chinese food and see how I was doing, and I told her that would be all right. Right now, though, I wanted to be alone. Alone to undress and crawl into my bed, pulling down the blinds and creeping like a wounded wild thing into my cocoon of blankets. I wanted to not think about this whole mess and I knew I was tired enough to do it.

I filled the cats' kibble bowls, apologized to them for being such a rotten mom, cast a doubtful eye on Repo and Pansy who were sitting on opposite arms of the couch ignoring each other, unplugged the phone, and dragged myself into the hall to my bedroom.

A ghostly green glow caught my eye. I didn't want to look. I knew my computer was on again, that another cryptic message would be displayed on the screen. But I just wasn't up to all the head-scratching required to figure it all out. To hell with it. I'd donate it to a nonprofit organization. Take a tax deduction.

As I strode into the room, intending to turn the computer off, a striped tabby head appeared from behind the monitor.

"Mmmmm?" Jeoffrey asked. Then he scratched,

and in a leisurely manner, walked across the keyboard. On the screen appeared:

???????lftyyyy[[[""""~~

"Huh?" I said.

With a *wuff* he lay down on the keys and rolling over, punched the POWER button with one paw. Instantly the screen blanked out.

"Ha!" I yelled, no doubt scaring the poor cat out of what remained of his ninth life. "So it was you all along, you striped technophile," I said, scooping him up and kissing him soundly. "Stay there, then," I told him, putting him back on the table. "Compute. Enjoy yourself." Through my pain and fatigue I felt a little glimmer of self-satisfaction. There's nothing like the solution to a mystery.

I yawned and continued into the bedroom, shedding clothes as I went. As I had suspected, I had hardly pulled on my sweats and tucked myself into bed when I was out. Like a snuffed candle. I might have groaned once as I tumbled into the embrace of sleep, but I wasn't sure. The last thought I had was about my guns. Tsk. Brendan would never approve. Sorry, I thought as I sank into oblivion. Sorry.

The pain in my head woke me and I sat up slowly, groggy, disoriented. Without putting on the light, I slowly swung my legs over the edge of the bed and stood upright. My head throbbed like hell and I suddenly remembered I had some codeine pills left over from my root canal. Gingerly I walked around the end of the bed and was just preparing to step into the bathroom when something in the hall caught my eye. A movement. I didn't think much of it. I waited, expecting to see one of the cats cross from the darkened hall to the lighter gloom of the kitchen. What I saw instead jolted me awake. A crouched human form slipped from the kitchen into the hall, hugging the wall in the darkness, making its way inexorably toward my bedroom.

Heart pounding, I recalled, too late, that both my guns were under my jacket in the living room. Well, I had an advantage this son of a bitch didn't have. Surprise. I knew he was coming. I stepped behind the bedroom door, held my breath, and waited. Through the crack between the door and the wall, I could see his stealthy approach. What made my hands sweat was that I could also see the gleam of a knife he held close to his body. Shit. I would have to time this just right.

He left the hall and crossed the threshold into my bedroom. I let him take one more slow step, two, three . . . and then I drew back my right leg and kicked as hard as I could, sending the door slamming into his body. I heard his cry of pain as he fell to the floor in the hall, gasping, and I tore open the door, not waiting to see how badly he was hurt. I vaulted his body and hit the floor running, rounded the corner of the living room, and made a dive for the couch. I had the familiar shape of my leather jacket between my hands in an instant and rolled off the couch, my .357 up and aimed. I knew I was at a disadvantage here on my knees, but I didn't have time to think about it. Because he was coming. At a dead run.

"Back off Macklin, you dumb shit," I yelled. "Whatever happened to you isn't worth dying for. You don't have to do this."

He gave no sign that he even heard me. Without breaking stride he raised the knife and threw himself at me. He made a splendid target leaping over the back of the couch. In fact, he seemed to hang in the air forever. I even had time to sight properly. I shot him twice in the body, just as I had been taught. He never had a chance. And that, I realized, was this particular intruder's intention. Too late, far too late, as the body collapsed onto the couch and its momentum carried it to the floor at my feet, a black knit cap slipped from its head and I saw the tangle of bright hair. Fox-colored hair. Cinnamon hair.

I ran to the window and wrenched the curtains open but I already knew what I would see. Still, I had to look. I had to be sure. Kneeling, I turned the body over.

Diana McNeil lay dead at my feet.

I sat down heavily and took one of her hands in mine. It was still warm. For no reason I could name, I held it to my cheek. Then, raising my head, I looked past the curtains I had opened out at the sky. It was sunset. The day that had begun for me at Gray's was almost over. Another day. Another chance. But not for Diana. Who the hell did I think I was, giving out chances? God?

I understood now what she had meant last night as we lay in bed together and she had asked me to forgive her for requiring me to be merciful. She wasn't asking me to exonerate her for her crimes; she was asking me to forgive her for making me kill her. No wonder I hadn't understood. I kissed her palm, and placed her hand back on the floor, just as it had been when she fell. Then I tried very hard to be angry. I had been *used*. Diana had aimed me like an arrow at this moment. It wasn't my fault. Dammit, if it was anyone's fault, it was hers, I told myself. Diana with her demons. Diana with that cryptic poem on her office door. Diana with her death wish.

"What do you want?" the boys had asked the Sibyl.

"I want to die," she had replied.

Well, she surely had. And I had killed her, promising not to hate her. What a monstrous burden she had placed on me. I felt guilty for even *trying* to feel anger.

I got up to make the necessary phone call. Then, because there was nothing I could do, I walked to the window and leaned my forehead against the cool glass. Grief and pain, I wanted the release of tears, but a perverse thought kept running through my head: for whom would I weep? For Diana, who had rid herself of the insupportable burden of life, or for myself, her dupe, the agent of her deliverance, her murderer?

CHAPTER THIRTEEN

Tonia arrived just as Sandy was pulling out of the driveway. The medical examiner's team had come and gone, the photographs had been taken, the reports had been filled out, and the body had been taken away. The body. Diana.

"C'mon in," I told Tonia brightly. "We'll have to eat in the kitchen, though. There's blood on the living room floor."

She gave me a wary look and carried the Chinese food in to the kitchen table. "Caitlin," she called when I didn't follow her. "Caitlin, what's wrong?" When I didn't answer, she looked at me curiously, then walked past me into the living room. "Oh, God, it is blood. What happened here?"

I leaned against the wall in the hall, trying to find the words to explain the terrible thing I had done. I couldn't think of any so I studied the wallpaper pattern.

She took off her jacket, tossed it over the back of the couch, and walked toward me. Touching the bandage over my ear, she commented, "You're bleeding."

I nodded, unable to meet her eyes. Indeed I was. In places she couldn't see, too.

She put two fingers under my chin and raised my head until I had to look at her. "Is that your blood in there?"

I shook my head slightly.

"Whose, then?"

I swallowed. "Diana McNeil's. I shot her."

She didn't flinch. "Tell me what happened," she said, reaching up to smooth my hair.

I shook my head again. "I . . . don't think I can. Not right now." To my immense embarrassment, my eyes filled with tears, which coursed in two hot streams down my cheeks. I dashed them away angrily.

"Jesus," Tonia breathed, reaching out and pulling me to her. I must have resisted, because Tonia said fiercely, "Let me hold you. Let me help you. Is that so damned hard?"

"Diana . . . she asked —"

"Diana later," she said, interrupting me. "She's dead. You're alive. Let's take care of you now."

A line from the poem I read at Gray's flashed

through my mind. What had the poet said? We make each other strong — that was it. Suddenly I understood.

She held me with surprising strength. "Go ahead," she said. "I'm here. I'll stay. I'll listen. I care."

I pulled my face away from her shoulder to look at her out of moisture-blurred eyes. "You do, don't you?" I said, amazed. I felt as though I had been given a great gift.

"Yes, I do. But for God's sake, cry, Caitlin! For both of you. For whatever Diana asked. It's all right. Cry."

So I did.

A few of the publications of
THE NAIAD PRESS, INC.
P.O. Box 10543 • Tallahassee, Florida 32302
Phone (904) 539-5965
Mail orders welcome. Please include 15% postage.

THE DAUGHTERS OF ARTEMIS by Lauren Wright Douglas.
240 pp. Third Caitlin Reece mystery.   ISBN 0-941483-95-9 $8.95

CLEARWATER by Catherine Ennis. 176 pp. Romantic secrets
of a small Louisiana town.   ISBN 0-941483-65-7   8.95

THE HALLELUJAH MURDERS by Dorothy Tell. 176 pp.
Second Poppy Dillworth mystery.   ISBN 0-941483-88-6   8.95

ZETA BASE by Judith Alguire. 208 pp. Lesbian triangle
on a future Earth.   ISBN 0-941483-94-0   9.95

SECOND CHANCE by Jackie Calhoun. 256 pp. Contemporary
Lesbian lives and loves.   ISBN 0-941483-93-2   9.95

MURDER BY TRADITION by Katherine V. Forrest. 288 pp.
A Kate Delafield Mystery. 4th in a series.   ISBN 0-941483-89-4   18.95

BENEDICTION by Diane Salvatore. 272 pp. Striking,
contemporary romantic novel.   ISBN 0-941483-90-8   9.95

CALLING RAIN by Karen Marie Christa Minns. 240 pp.
Spellbinding, erotic love story   ISBN 0-941483-87-8   9.95

BLACK IRIS by Jeane Harris. 192 pp. Caroline's hidden past . . .
ISBN 0-941483-68-1   8.95

TOUCHWOOD by Karin Kallmaker. 240 pp. Loving, May/
December romance.   ISBN 0-941483-76-2   8.95

BAYOU CITY SECRETS by Deborah Powell. 224 pp. A Hollis
Carpenter mystery. First in a series.   ISBN 0-941483-91-6   8.95

COP OUT by Claire McNab. 208 pp. 4th Det. Insp. Carol Ashton
mystery.   ISBN 0-941483-84-3   8.95

LODESTAR by Phyllis Horn. 224 pp. Romantic, fast-moving
adventure.   ISBN 0-941483-83-5   8.95

THE BEVERLY MALIBU by Katherine V. Forrest. 288 pp. A
Kate Delafield Mystery. 3rd in a series. (HC)   ISBN 0-941483-47-9   16.95
                    Paperback   ISBN 0-941483-48-7   9.95

THAT OLD STUDEBAKER by Lee Lynch. 272 pp. Andy's affair
with Regina and her attachment to her beloved car.
ISBN 0-941483-82-7   9.95

PASSION'S LEGACY by Lori Paige. 224 pp. Sarah is swept into
the arms of Augusta Pym in this delightful historical romance.
ISBN 0-941483-81-9   8.95

THE PROVIDENCE FILE by Amanda Kyle Williams. 256 pp.
Second espionage thriller featuring lesbian agent Madison McGuire
ISBN 0-941483-92-4   8.95

I LEFT MY HEART by Jaye Maiman. 320 pp. A Robin Miller
Mystery. First in a series.   ISBN 0-941483-72-X   9.95

THE PRICE OF SALT by Patricia Highsmith (writing as Claire
Morgan). 288 pp. Classic lesbian novel, first issued in 1952 . . .
acknowledged by its author under her own, very famous, name.
ISBN 1-56280-003-5   8.95

SIDE BY SIDE by Isabel Miller. 256 pp. From beloved author of
Patience and Sarah.   ISBN 0-941483-77-0   8.95

SOUTHBOUND by Sheila Ortiz Taylor. 240 pp. Hilarious sequel
to *Faultline*.   ISBN 0-941483-78-9   8.95

STAYING POWER: LONG TERM LESBIAN COUPLES
by Susan E. Johnson. 352 pp. Joys of coupledom.
ISBN 0-941-483-75-4   12.95

SLICK by Camarin Grae. 304 pp. Exotic, erotic adventure.
ISBN 0-941483-74-6   9.95

NINTH LIFE by Lauren Wright Douglas. 256 pp. A Caitlin
Reece mystery. 2nd in a series.   ISBN 0-941483-50-9   8.95

PLAYERS by Robbi Sommers. 192 pp. Sizzling, erotic novel.
ISBN 0-941483-73-8   8.95

MURDER AT RED ROOK RANCH by Dorothy Tell. 224 pp.
First Poppy Dillworth adventure.   ISBN 0-941483-80-0   8.95

LESBIAN SURVIVAL MANUAL by Rhonda Dicksion.
112 pp. Cartoons!   ISBN 0-941483-71-1   8.95

A ROOM FULL OF WOMEN by Elisabeth Nonas. 256 pp.
Contemporary Lesbian lives.   ISBN 0-941483-69-X   8.95

MURDER IS RELATIVE by Karen Saum. 256 pp. The first
Brigid Donovan mystery.   ISBN 0-941483-70-3   8.95

PRIORITIES by Lynda Lyons 288 pp. Science fiction with
a twist.   ISBN 0-941483-66-5   8.95

THEME FOR DIVERSE INSTRUMENTS by Jane Rule. 208
pp. Powerful romantic lesbian stories.   ISBN 0-941483-63-0   8.95

LESBIAN QUERIES by Hertz & Ertman. 112 pp. The questions
you were too embarrassed to ask.   ISBN 0-941483-67-3   8.95

CLUB 12 by Amanda Kyle Williams. 288 pp. Espionage thriller
featuring a lesbian agent!   ISBN 0-941483-64-9   8.95

DEATH DOWN UNDER by Claire McNab. 240 pp. 3rd Det.
Insp. Carol Ashton mystery.   ISBN 0-941483-39-8   8.95

MONTANA FEATHERS by Penny Hayes. 256 pp. Vivian and
Elizabeth find love in frontier Montana.   ISBN 0-941483-61-4   8.95

CHESAPEAKE PROJECT by Phyllis Horn. 304 pp. Jessie &
Meredith in perilous adventure.   ISBN 0-941483-58-4   8.95

LIFESTYLES by Jackie Calhoun. 224 pp. Contemporary Lesbian
lives and loves.   ISBN 0-941483-57-6   8.95

VIRAGO by Karen Marie Christa Minns. 208 pp. Darsen has
chosen Ginny.   ISBN 0-941483-56-8   8.95

WILDERNESS TREK by Dorothy Tell. 192 pp. Six women on
vacation learning "new" skills.   ISBN 0-941483-60-6   8.95

MURDER BY THE BOOK by Pat Welch. 256 pp. A Helen
Black Mystery. First in a series.   ISBN 0-941483-59-2   8.95

BERRIGAN by Vicki P. McConnell. 176 pp. Youthful Lesbian —
romantic, idealistic Berrigan.   ISBN 0-941483-55-X   8.95

LESBIANS IN GERMANY by Lillian Faderman & B. Eriksson.
128 pp. Fiction, poetry, essays.   ISBN 0-941483-62-2   8.95

THERE'S SOMETHING I'VE BEEN MEANING TO TELL
YOU Ed. by Loralee MacPike. 288 pp. Gay men and lesbians
coming out to their children.   ISBN 0-941483-44-4   9.95
                                          ISBN 0-941483-54-1   16.95

LIFTING BELLY by Gertrude Stein. Ed. by Rebecca Mark. 104
pp. Erotic poetry.   ISBN 0-941483-51-7   8.95
                                          ISBN 0-941483-53-3   14.95

ROSE PENSKI by Roz Perry. 192 pp. Adult lovers in a long-term
relationship.   ISBN 0-941483-37-1   8.95

AFTER THE FIRE by Jane Rule. 256 pp. Warm, human novel
by this incomparable author.   ISBN 0-941483-45-2   8.95

SUE SLATE, PRIVATE EYE by Lee Lynch. 176 pp. The gay
folk of Peacock Alley are all cats.   ISBN 0-941483-52-5   8.95

CHRIS by Randy Salem. 224 pp. Golden oldie. Handsome Chris
and her adventures.   ISBN 0-941483-42-8   8.95

THREE WOMEN by March Hastings. 232 pp. Golden oldie. A
triangle among wealthy sophisticates.   ISBN 0-941483-43-6   8.95

RICE AND BEANS by Valeria Taylor. 232 pp. Love and
romance on poverty row.   ISBN 0-941483-41-X   8.95

PLEASURES by Robbi Sommers. 204 pp. Unprecedented
eroticism.   ISBN 0-941483-49-5   8.95

EDGEWISE by Camarin Grae. 372 pp. Spellbinding
adventure.   ISBN 0-941483-19-3   9.95

FATAL REUNION by Claire McNab. 224 pp. 2nd Det. Inspec.
Carol Ashton mystery.   ISBN 0-941483-40-1   8.95

KEEP TO ME STRANGER by Sarah Aldridge. 372 pp. Romance
set in a department store dynasty.   ISBN 0-941483-38-X   9.95

HEARTSCAPE by Sue Gambill. 204 pp. American lesbian in
Portugal.   ISBN 0-941483-33-9   8.95

IN THE BLOOD by Lauren Wright Douglas. 252 pp. Lesbian
science fiction adventure fantasy   ISBN 0-941483-22-3   8.95

THE BEE'S KISS by Shirley Verel. 216 pp. Delicate, delicious
romance.   ISBN 0-941483-36-3   8.95

RAGING MOTHER MOUNTAIN by Pat Emmerson. 264 pp.
Furosa Firechild's adventures in Wonderland.   ISBN 0-941483-35-5   8.95

IN EVERY PORT by Karin Kallmaker. 228 pp. Jessica's sexy,
adventuresome travels.   ISBN 0-941483-37-7   8.95

OF LOVE AND GLORY by Evelyn Kennedy. 192 pp. Exciting
WWII romance.   ISBN 0-941483-32-0   8.95

CLICKING STONES by Nancy Tyler Glenn. 288 pp. Love
transcending time.   ISBN 0-941483-31-2   9.95

SURVIVING SISTERS by Gail Pass. 252 pp. Powerful love
story.   ISBN 0-941483-16-9   8.95

SOUTH OF THE LINE by Catherine Ennis. 216 pp. Civil War
adventure.   ISBN 0-941483-29-0   8.95

WOMAN PLUS WOMAN by Dolores Klaich. 300 pp. Supurb
Lesbian overview.   ISBN 0-941483-28-2   9.95

SLOW DANCING AT MISS POLLY'S by Sheila Ortiz Taylor.
96 pp. Lesbian Poetry   ISBN 0-941483-30-4   7.95

DOUBLE DAUGHTER by Vicki P. McConnell. 216 pp. A Nyla
Wade Mystery, third in the series.   ISBN 0-941483-26-6   8.95

HEAVY GILT by Delores Klaich. 192 pp. Lesbian detective/
disappearing homophobes/upper class gay society.
                                                ISBN 0-941483-25-8   8.95

THE FINER GRAIN by Denise Ohio. 216 pp. Brilliant young
college lesbian novel.   ISBN 0-941483-11-8   8.95

THE AMAZON TRAIL by Lee Lynch. 216 pp. Life, travel & lore
of famous lesbian author.   ISBN 0-941483-27-4   8.95

HIGH CONTRAST by Jessie Lattimore. 264 pp. Women of the
Crystal Palace.   ISBN 0-941483-17-7   8.95

OCTOBER OBSESSION by Meredith More. Josie's rich, secret
Lesbian life.   ISBN 0-941483-18-5   8.95

LESBIAN CROSSROADS by Ruth Baetz. 276 pp. Contemporary
Lesbian lives.   ISBN 0-941483-21-5   9.95

BEFORE STONEWALL: THE MAKING OF A GAY AND
LESBIAN COMMUNITY by Andrea Weiss & Greta Schiller.
96 pp., 25 illus.   ISBN 0-941483-20-7   7.95

WE WALK THE BACK OF THE TIGER by Patricia A. Murphy.
192 pp. Romantic Lesbian novel/beginning women's movement.
                                ISBN 0-941483-13-4   8.95

SUNDAY'S CHILD by Joyce Bright. 216 pp. Lesbian athletics, at
last the novel about sports.   ISBN 0-941483-12-6   8.95

OSTEN'S BAY by Zenobia N. Vole. 204 pp. Sizzling adventure
romance set on Bonaire.   ISBN 0-941483-15-0   8.95

LESSONS IN MURDER by Claire McNab. 216 pp. 1st Det. Inspec.
Carol Ashton mystery — erotic tension!.   ISBN 0-941483-14-2   8.95

YELLOWTHROAT by Penny Hayes. 240 pp. Margarita, bandit,
kidnaps Julia.   ISBN 0-941483-10-X   8.95

SAPPHISTRY: THE BOOK OF LESBIAN SEXUALITY by
Pat Califia. 3d edition, revised. 208 pp.   ISBN 0-941483-24-X   8.95

CHERISHED LOVE by Evelyn Kennedy. 192 pp. Erotic
Lesbian love story.   ISBN 0-941483-08-8   8.95

LAST SEPTEMBER by Helen R. Hull. 208 pp. Six stories & a
glorious novella.   ISBN 0-941483-09-6   8.95

THE SECRET IN THE BIRD by Camarin Grae. 312 pp. Striking,
psychological suspense novel.   ISBN 0-941483-05-3   8.95

TO THE LIGHTNING by Catherine Ennis. 208 pp. Romantic
Lesbian 'Robinson Crusoe' adventure.   ISBN 0-941483-06-1   8.95

THE OTHER SIDE OF VENUS by Shirley Verel. 224 pp.
Luminous, romantic love story.   ISBN 0-941483-07-X   8.95

DREAMS AND SWORDS by Katherine V. Forrest. 192 pp.
Romantic, erotic, imaginative stories.   ISBN 0-941483-03-7   8.95

MEMORY BOARD by Jane Rule. 336 pp. Memorable novel
about an aging Lesbian couple.   ISBN 0-941483-02-9   9.95

THE ALWAYS ANONYMOUS BEAST by Lauren Wright
Douglas. 224 pp. A Caitlin Reece mystery. First in a series.
                                ISBN 0-941483-04-5   8.95

SEARCHING FOR SPRING by Patricia A. Murphy. 224 pp.
Novel about the recovery of love.   ISBN 0-941483-00-2   8.95

DUSTY'S QUEEN OF HEARTS DINER by Lee Lynch. 240 pp.
Romantic blue-collar novel.   ISBN 0-941483-01-0   8.95

PARENTS MATTER by Ann Muller. 240 pp. Parents'
relationships with Lesbian daughters and gay sons.
                                ISBN 0-930044-91-6   9.95

THE PEARLS by Shelley Smith. 176 pp. Passion and fun in
the Caribbean sun.   ISBN 0-930044-93-2   7.95

MAGDALENA by Sarah Aldridge. 352 pp. Epic Lesbian novel
set on three continents.   ISBN 0-930044-99-1   8.95

THE BLACK AND WHITE OF IT by Ann Allen Shockley.
144 pp. Short stories.   ISBN 0-930044-96-7   7.95

SAY JESUS AND COME TO ME by Ann Allen Shockley. 288
pp. Contemporary romance.   ISBN 0-930044-98-3   8.95

LOVING HER by Ann Allen Shockley. 192 pp. Romantic love
story.   ISBN 0-930044-97-5   7.95

MURDER AT THE NIGHTWOOD BAR by Katherine V.
Forrest. 240 pp. A Kate Delafield mystery. Second in a series.
                                       ISBN 0-930044-92-4   8.95

ZOE'S BOOK by Gail Pass. 224 pp. Passionate, obsessive love
story.   ISBN 0-930044-95-9   7.95

WINGED DANCER by Camarin Grae. 228 pp. Erotic Lesbian
adventure story.   ISBN 0-930044-88-6   8.95

PAZ by Camarin Grae. 336 pp. Romantic Lesbian adventurer
with the power to change the world.   ISBN 0-930044-89-4   8.95

SOUL SNATCHER by Camarin Grae. 224 pp. A puzzle, an
adventure, a mystery — Lesbian romance. ISBN 0-930044-90-8   8.95

THE LOVE OF GOOD WOMEN by Isabel Miller. 224 pp.
Long-awaited new novel by the author of the beloved *Patience
and Sarah*.   ISBN 0-930044-81-9   8.95

THE HOUSE AT PELHAM FALLS by Brenda Weathers. 240
pp. Suspenseful Lesbian ghost story.   ISBN 0-930044-79-7   7.95

HOME IN YOUR HANDS by Lee Lynch. 240 pp. More stories
from the author of *Old Dyke Tales*.   ISBN 0-930044-80-0   7.95

EACH HAND A MAP by Anita Skeen. 112 pp. Real-life poems
that touch us all.   ISBN 0-930044-82-7   6.95

SURPLUS by Sylvia Stevenson. 342 pp. A classic early Lesbian
novel.   ISBN 0-930044-78-9   7.95

PEMBROKE PARK by Michelle Martin. 256 pp. Derring-do
and daring romance in Regency England. ISBN 0-930044-77-0   7.95

THE LONG TRAIL by Penny Hayes. 248 pp. Vivid adventures
of two women in love in the old west. ISBN 0-930044-76-2   8.95

HORIZON OF THE HEART by Shelley Smith. 192 pp. Hot
romance in summertime New England.   ISBN 0-930044-75-4   7.95

AN EMERGENCE OF GREEN by Katherine V. Forrest. 288
pp. Powerful novel of sexual discovery. ISBN 0-930044-69-X   9.95

THE LESBIAN PERIODICALS INDEX edited by Claire
Potter. 432 pp. Author & subject index. ISBN 0-930044-74-6   29.95

DESERT OF THE HEART by Jane Rule. 224 pp. A classic; basis for the movie *Desert Hearts*. ISBN 0-930044-73-8   8.95

SPRING FORWARD/FALL BACK by Sheila Ortiz Taylor. 288 pp. Literary novel of timeless love. ISBN 0-930044-70-3   7.95

FOR KEEPS by Elisabeth Nonas. 144 pp. Contemporary novel about losing and finding love. ISBN 0-930044-71-1   7.95

TORCHLIGHT TO VALHALLA by Gale Wilhelm. 128 pp. Classic novel by a great Lesbian writer. ISBN 0-930044-68-1   7.95

LESBIAN NUNS: BREAKING SILENCE edited by Rosemary Curb and Nancy Manahan. 432 pp. Unprecedented autobiographies of religious life. ISBN 0-930044-62-2   9.95

THE SWASHBUCKLER by Lee Lynch. 288 pp. Colorful novel set in Greenwich Village in the sixties. ISBN 0-930044-66-5   8.95

MISFORTUNE'S FRIEND by Sarah Aldridge. 320 pp. Historical Lesbian novel set on two continents. ISBN 0-930044-67-3   7.95

A STUDIO OF ONE'S OWN by Ann Stokes. Edited by Dolores Klaich. 128 pp. Autobiography. ISBN 0-930044-64-9   7.95

SEX VARIANT WOMEN IN LITERATURE by Jeannette Howard Foster. 448 pp. Literary history. ISBN 0-930044-65-7   8.95

A HOT-EYED MODERATE by Jane Rule. 252 pp. Hard-hitting essays on gay life; writing; art. ISBN 0-930044-57-6   7.95

INLAND PASSAGE AND OTHER STORIES by Jane Rule. 288 pp. Wide-ranging new collection. ISBN 0-930044-56-8   7.95

WE TOO ARE DRIFTING by Gale Wilhelm. 128 pp. Timeless Lesbian novel, a masterpiece. ISBN 0-930044-61-4   6.95

AMATEUR CITY by Katherine V. Forrest. 224 pp. A Kate Delafield mystery. First in a series. ISBN 0-930044-55-X   8.95

THE SOPHIE HOROWITZ STORY by Sarah Schulman. 176 pp. Engaging novel of madcap intrigue. ISBN 0-930044-54-1   7.95

THE BURNTON WIDOWS by Vickie P. McConnell. 272 pp. A Nyla Wade mystery, second in the series. ISBN 0-930044-52-5   7.95

OLD DYKE TALES by Lee Lynch. 224 pp. Extraordinary stories of our diverse Lesbian lives. ISBN 0-930044-51-7   8.95

DAUGHTERS OF A CORAL DAWN by Katherine V. Forrest. 240 pp. Novel set in a Lesbian new world. ISBN 0-930044-50-9   8.95

AGAINST THE SEASON by Jane Rule. 224 pp. Luminous, complex novel of interrelationships. ISBN 0-930044-48-7   8.95

LOVERS IN THE PRESENT AFTERNOON by Kathleen Fleming. 288 pp. A novel about recovery and growth. ISBN 0-930044-46-0   8.95

TOOTHPICK HOUSE by Lee Lynch. 264 pp. Love between
two Lesbians of different classes.   ISBN 0-930044-45-2   7.95

MADAME AURORA by Sarah Aldridge. 256 pp. Historical
novel featuring a charismatic "seer."   ISBN 0-930044-44-4   7.95

CURIOUS WINE by Katherine V. Forrest. 176 pp. Passionate
Lesbian love story, a best-seller.   ISBN 0-930044-43-6   8.95

BLACK LESBIAN IN WHITE AMERICA by Anita Cornwell.
141 pp. Stories, essays, autobiography.   ISBN 0-930044-41-X   7.95

CONTRACT WITH THE WORLD by Jane Rule. 340 pp.
Powerful, panoramic novel of gay life.   ISBN 0-930044-28-2   9.95

MRS. PORTER'S LETTER by Vicki P. McConnell. 224 pp.
The first Nyla Wade mystery.   ISBN 0-930044-29-0   7.95

TO THE CLEVELAND STATION by Carol Anne Douglas.
192 pp. Interracial Lesbian love story.   ISBN 0-930044-27-4   6.95

THE NESTING PLACE by Sarah Aldridge. 224 pp. A
three-woman triangle — love conquers all!   ISBN 0-930044-26-6   7.95

THIS IS NOT FOR YOU by Jane Rule. 284 pp. A letter to a
beloved is also an intricate novel.   ISBN 0-930044-25-8   8.95

FAULTLINE by Sheila Ortiz Taylor. 140 pp. Warm, funny,
literate story of a startling family.   ISBN 0-930044-24-X   6.95

ANNA'S COUNTRY by Elizabeth Lang. 208 pp. A woman
finds her Lesbian identity.   ISBN 0-930044-19-3   8.95

PRISM by Valerie Taylor. 158 pp. A love affair between two
women in their sixties.   ISBN 0-930044-18-5   6.95

THE MARQUISE AND THE NOVICE by Victoria Ramstetter.
108 pp. A Lesbian Gothic novel.   ISBN 0-930044-16-9   6.95

OUTLANDER by Jane Rule. 207 pp. Short stories and essays
by one of our finest writers.   ISBN 0-930044-17-7   8.95

ALL TRUE LOVERS by Sarah Aldridge. 292 pp. Romantic
novel set in the 1930s and 1940s.   ISBN 0-930044-10-X   8.95

A WOMAN APPEARED TO ME by Renee Vivien. 65 pp. A
classic; translated by Jeannette H. Foster.   ISBN 0-930044-06-1   5.00

CYTHEREA'S BREATH by Sarah Aldridge. 240 pp. Romantic
novel about women's entrance into medicine.
                                           ISBN 0-930044-02-9   6.95

TOTTIE by Sarah Aldridge. 181 pp. Lesbian romance in the
turmoil of the sixties.   ISBN 0-930044-01-0   6.95

THE LATECOMER by Sarah Aldridge. 107 pp. A delicate love
story.   ISBN 0-930044-00-2   6.95

ODD GIRL OUT by Ann Bannon.   ISBN 0-930044-83-5   5.95
I AM A WOMAN 84-3; WOMEN IN THE SHADOWS 85-1;   each
JOURNEY TO A WOMAN 86-X; BEEBO BRINKER 87-8. Golden
oldies about life in Greenwich Village.

JOURNEY TO FULFILLMENT, A WORLD WITHOUT MEN, and   3.95
RETURN TO LESBOS. All by Valerie Taylor   each

These are just a few of the many Naiad Press titles — we are the oldest and
largest lesbian/feminist publishing company in the world. Please request a
complete catalog. We offer personal service; we encourage and welcome direct
mail orders from individuals who have limited access to bookstores carrying
our publications.